The Non-Stop Connolly Show
Part Four

First published 1978 by Pluto Press Limited
Unit 10 Spencer Court, 7 Chalcot Road, London NW1 8LH

ISBN 0 904383 82 2

Designed by Tom Sullivan
Cover designed by Kate Hepburn
Cover photo: from the London production of
The Non-Stop Connolly Show at the Almost Free Theatre,
by Tom Hutcheson for Inter-Action Limited
Printed in Great Britain by Latimer Trend & Company Ltd Plymouth

Margaretta D'Arcy and John Arden

The Non-Stop Connolly Show
A Dramatic Cycle of Continuous
Struggle in Six Parts

Part Four:
The New World 1903–1910

Pluto  Plays

To the memory of Liam MacMillen of the Belfast Republican
Clubs, whose vigour and enthusiasm made possible
The Non-Stop Connolly Show in that city: and who was shot
dead in the street only a few days after we had played there.

Margaretta D'Arcy and John Arden

NOTES ON THE AUTHORS:

Margaretta D'Arcy comes from Dublin, where she obtained her early
experience in the theatre. She has worked in the theatre consistently since
1951. Co-author of sixteen scripts for stage, radio and TV. Presently lives in
Galway, where she is involved with experimental community
workshop-theatre. She is currently preparing, with Patricia Cobey, a book
on women in contemporary Ireland to be published by Virago; and her
play *A Pinprick of History*, dealing with the 1977 Irish general election, was
recently produced at the Almost Free Theatre.

John Arden was born in Barnsley, Yorkshire. Began full-time theatre
writing in 1958 for the Royal Court, London. Author of *Serjeant
Musgrave's Dance*, *Armstrong's Last Goodnight*, etc. A collection of essays
on the theatre, *To Present The Pretence*, has recently been published by
Eyre Methuen. Forthcoming work includes a radio play, *Pearl*.

AUTHORS' PREFACE

James Connolly holds a unique place in early twentieth-century European history. He was the only revolutionary leader of his time who combined in his career:

– genuine proletarian origins
– a consistent record of work amongst the international socialist movement in several countries (Britain, Ireland, America)
– continuous involvement with trade-union organisations as well as revolutionary political parties
– opposition to the national hysteria of the first world war, which engulfed so much of the international labour-leadership
– practical physical expression of that opposition, in that he was one of the chief organisers of the Dublin Rising of 1916.

Throughout his career, and closely interwoven with each of the above aspects of his life, one can trace the recurrent conflict between *revolution* and *reform* – an ideological dichotomy that still plagues all who have ever had anything to do with left-wing political affairs. In Connolly's case this prolonged debate took on so many shapes and faces that we felt it necessary to explore his experience at deliberately repetitive length – hence a cycle of plays rather than one clean-cut three-act summary. Other recurrent themes that lift their coils in and out of the story, like the serpents' bodies in an old Celtic manuscript-ornament, are:

– the perennial failure of the British Left to recognise and cope with the imperialist role of Britain in relation to Ireland
– the confusion among international socialism caused by the national independence movements in such colonial and semi-colonial countries as Ireland, Poland, Serbia, etc.

These six plays have therefore taken the form of not so much a straight biography of Connolly, as a series of digressive stage-presentations of the events of his time which influenced his political views and consequent actions. They were written to be shown as one complete connected sequence, and have been so produced, both in Dublin and in London. There were certain differences of emphasis between the two productions.

In Dublin our aim was primarily to counteract what one might term the 'Conor Cruise O'Brien historical revisionism', currently much in vogue in Irish intellectual circles, and closely associated with the policies of the Fine Gael-Labour Coalition government – in which Dr Cruise O'Brien was himself a minister. This school of thought appears to maintain:

– that the 1916 Rising was unnecessary
– that Irish Independence would have been achieved anyway through constitutional parliamentary processes
– that the Protestant-Loyalist minority in Ireland (which forms a *majority* in six of the counties of Ulster) is in effect a nation of its own, quite distinct from the rest of the Irish population

– that the present anti-imperialist struggle in the country has therefore no historical validity.

To reinforce these theoretical opinions in the Irish Republic, successive governments (both Fianna Fail and Coalition) have made use of a whole series of repressive measures – including:

– trials for political offences before a Special Court without a jury

– official censorship of radio and television broadcasts

– self-censorship of the press under threat of government interference

– imprisonment of citizens upon no stronger evidence than the unsupported word of a senior police-officer that he *believes* them to be 'subversives'

– the 1976 declaration of a State of Emergency to give extra powers to the Army 'in support of the civil authority', and to permit the police to hold persons on suspicion for seven days before bringing them before a court.

Amnesty International has investigated the state of the Irish prisons: and the new Fianna Fail government has been compelled to re-examine the situation. It also appears (5 October 1977) that the seven-day detention system is likely to be shelved, as a result of widespread public disquiet.

The London production of the plays, on the other hand, was intended to demonstrate how the unwillingness of the Labour Movement in Britain to take a firm stand in support of Irish self-determination has resulted throughout several generations in a strengthening of the Anglo-Irish reactionary elements, which in turn has meant the augmentation of violence, bloodshed and widespread public suffering – a process which shows no signs of decrease. This lack of cross-channel awareness and solidarity has been directly responsible for IRA bombings in Britain, with the consequent Prevention of Terrorism Act, the censorship and crypto-censorship of Irish themes in all departments of the British media, the deportation of large numbers of Irish people without adequate means of defence, the maltreatment of Irish political prisoners in British gaols etc. etc ... The latter point is to be taken up at Strasburg – where the army and police torture-policy in Ulster has already been proven*– but the political impact of such revelations upon the broad British Left has, at the time of writing, been negligible.

NOTES ON THE STAGING OF THE PLAYS

Despite the apparent complexity of *The Non-Stop Connolly Show*, its staging need not present any very difficult problems. The approach should be 'emblematic' rather than 'naturalistic'; and ideally a number of stages should be used, arranged around the audience, and connected perhaps with gangways at various levels. We have suggested a series of backcloths which can be fixed either singly or two-at-a-time to give the overall atmosphere of each section of the cycle.

* The European Human Rights Court judgement of 18 January 1978 draws a distinction between *torture* and *inhuman degrading treatment*, acquitting the British government of the former. We do not regard this as more than a semantic quibble.

The large cast can be contained by a basic company of about a dozen actors, who will each have to play many different roles, not necessarily of their own sex: but stylised, easily-changed, strongly-defined costumes, and possibly stock-masks for recurrent social types (i.e. bourgeois politicians, employers, military officers, etc.), would greatly assist this technique.

The part of Connolly does not necessarily have to be played by the same actor in all six parts. It might be difficult to find an artist capable of handling him all the way through from childhood to middle-age – but that this taxing feat of character portrayal is possible was proven in Dublin by the remarkable performance of Terry McGinity, who came into the production halfway through rehearsals and became, we are convinced, truly possessed by the dead hero's *daimon*.

The music for the songs in the Dublin and London productions was found from traditional sources—there are many Irish, British and American airs which will fit the words – and we employed an improvised accompaniment, largely percussive, to give accent to the stage movement and the delivery of some of the more rhetorical dialogue and tirade.

The backcloths are described in the text. The style we have in mind should be based on the formal emblematic tradition of trade union banners, and should be carried out in bright colours with no attempt at impressionism or naturalistic representation. The cloths should include appropriate slogans and captions.

Essentially the plays need *speed* – and close attention to *rhythm*. Each scene or episode should be understood as a self-contained combination of voice, movement, colour and music, with a precise dramatic momentum of its own, which makes its point as sharply as possible and is then withdrawn from the stage, as sharply as possible, to be replaced by the next grouping. We would emphasise finally that the play will work only if the actors are more concerned with understanding the political arguments and implications of the story than with 'creating character' in the normal theatrical sense. A few books which could be usefully referred to for this purpose, as well as the works of James Connolly:

C. Desmond Greaves, *The Life and Times of James Connolly*, Lawrence & Wishart.
T. A. Jackson, *Ireland Her Own*, Lawrence & Wishart.
George Dangerfield, *The Strange Death of Liberal England*, MacGibbon & Kee.
Ray Ginger, *Eugene V. Debs*, Collier Books.
Richard M. Watt, *The Kings Depart*, Penguin Books.
James Connolly, *Selected Writings*, ed. by Peter Beresford, Penguin.
Jack Gale, *Oppression and Revolt in Ireland*, Workers' Revolutionary Party Pocket Book No. 15.

The Non-Stop Connolly Show received its first production in Dublin, at Liberty Hall (headquarters of the Irish Transport and General Workers' Union) on Easter weekend, Saturday–Sunday, 29/30 March 1975

Cast

    Connolly Terence J. McGinity

    Larkin Gerry O'Leary

    De Leon Barrie Houghton

Other parts were played by:

Paschal Finnan	Frank Macken
Niamh Fitzgerald	Vincent McCabe
Don Foley	Dave McKenna
Meryl Gourlay	Kevin McKenna
Des Hogan	Fionnuala Rogerson
Boris Howarth	Sandra Rudkin
Margaret Howarth	Paddy Scully
Garret Kehoe	

together with the following members of the Irish Workers' Cultural Centre:

Mildred Fleming	Sheila Moran
Maura Heffernan	Virginia O'Reilly
Paul McGrath	Eamon Walsh
Mick Moran	

Children's parts were played by:

    Members of na Fianna Éireann

    Finn Arden

    Jacob Arden

    Neuss Arden

    During the subsequent tour of the production in Ireland the part of **Connolly** as a boy was played by Neuss Arden.

The direction of the production was co-ordinated by:

    John Arden

    Margaretta D'Arcy

    Jim Sheridan

    Robert Walker

who were also members of the cast.

Others involved in the general administration and preparation of the production:

Senator Michael Mullen and the General Executive Committee ITGWU, Premises Manager and Staff of Liberty Hall, Eoghan Harris, Tom Kilroy, Des Geraghty, Peter Sheridan, Paddy Gillan, Brian Flynn, Tomas Mac Giolla, Mairin de Burca, Tony Ebbes, Bill Whelan, Eric Fleming, Eamonn Travers, Eamonn Smullen, Cathal Goulding, Cathal Og Goulding, Paula, Niall Stokes, Joe Deasy, Margaret Gaj, The Union of Students in Ireland, Jim Nolan, Students Representative Council UCD, Jim Campbell, Des O'Hagan, Bronwen Casson, Norah Lever, Sean Byrne, Raymond Flynn, Felicia McCabe, Ottavio di Fidio . . . and many more.

The production was sponsored by the Irish Transport and General Workers' Union and the Official Sinn Fein Party.

The London presentation of *The Non-Stop Connolly Show* was produced by Inter-action Ltd at the Almost Free Theatre, as a series of rehearsed readings at lunch time, from 17 May–19 June 1976, under the direction of the authors, with a cast recruited in England.

Part Four: The New World 1903–1910

Act One: 'Into the Party'. James Connolly emigrates to the United States. He joins the Socialist Labor Party, led by Daniel De Leon. He is frustrated by its doctrinaire sectarianism.

List of characters:

JAMES CONNOLLY
LILLIE CONNOLLY

EUGENE DEBS

DANIEL DE LEON
MANAGER of De Leon's newspaper office
PASSANO (Branch Secretary, Socialist Labor Party)
3 Socialist Labor Party MEMBERS (Troy Branch)
Socialist Labor Party Conference CHAIRMAN

WOMAN WORKER

WILLIAM HAYWOOD
MOTHER JONES
2 MINERS

SAMUEL GOMPERS

GRABITALL
3 BOSSES
MANAGER of Insurance Company
2 DETECTIVES
3 Immigration OFFICIALS

immigrant workers, newspaper-office staff, children, shirt-factory women, newsboys, Socialist Labor Party Conference delegates, etc.

Act Two: 'Out of the Party'. James Connolly greets with enthusiasm the Industrial Workers of the World, believing them to be the great new revolutionary force. He forms the Irish Socialist Federation among immigrants to the USA. Unable to accommodate himself to De Leon's control of the Socialist Labor Party, he determines to pursue his politics elsewhere.

List of characters:
JAMES CONNOLLY
LILLIE CONNOLLY
NORA CONNOLLY (their daughter)

EUGENE DEBS

DANIEL DE LEON
3 Socialist Labor Party OFFICIALS
Socialist Labor Party COMMITTEE SECRETARY

ELIZABETH GURLEY FLYNN
Irish-American PARTY WORKER (SLP)
Industrial Workers of the World ORGANISER
2 HOBOES

RUSSIAN REVOLUTIONARY EXILE
FENIAN REVOLUTIONARY EXILE

WILLIAM HAYWOOD
MOYER
PETTIBONE
MOTHER JONES

SAMUEL GOMPERS
2 AMERICAN FEDERATION OF LABOR (AF of L) OFFICIALS
AF of L OFFICIAL (Newark)

GRABITALL
3 BOSSES
MANAGER of Sewing-Machine Company
SECRETARY of Sewing-Machine Company
SUPERVISOR of Sewing-Machine Company
Irish-American PUBLICAN
POLICE OFFICER
PEACE-OFFICER
PINKERTON DETECTIVE

2 REPORTERS
LIBRARY ASSISTANT
DOCTOR

hoboes, socialists, demonstrators, Wobblies, police, Irish-Americans, newsboys, etc.

Act Three: 'Forward to the revolution . . . ?' James Connolly, as IWW
Organiser, struggles against odds in New York. He helps the presidential
election campaign of Eugene Debs. He becomes a paid worker for the
Socialist Party of America. He determines to go elsewhere.

List of characters:
JAMES CONNOLLY
LILLIE CONNOLLY
NORA CONNOLLY (their daughter)

EUGENE DEBS
HILLQUIT
3 MEMBERS of the Socialist Party of America

DANIEL DE LEON
Socialist Labor Party OFFICIAL

WILLIAM HAYWOOD
ELIZABETH GURLEY FLYNN
CHAIRMAN of IWW meeting (New York)
CHAIRMAN of IWW National Convention
3 DELEGATES to IWW meeting (New York)
IWW OFFICIAL

JAMES LARKIN

SAMUEL GOMPERS
AF of L OFFICIAL (Construction Union)
AF of L OFFICIAL (Teamsters Union)

GRABITALL
3 BOSSES
Irish-American PUBLICAN
CARDINAL-ARCHBISHOP of Armagh
POLICE OFFICER
HOODLUM
BUILDING FOREMAN

2 Building WORKERS
2 REPORTERS
IRISH IMMIGRANT

A letter from Ireland

unemployed, hoodlums, female garment workers, tramway workers, police,
Socialist Party workers, IWW delegates, US Marines etc.

Part Four: The New World

ACT 1: Into the Party

SCENE 1

Immigrants arriving in the USA from a ship; with the Statue of Liberty, watchful police, and skyscrapers filling the background, so that little or no sky is visible. (Backcloth 6.)

The wide open spaces of America, mountain, desert and farmland, with groups of workers with red flags confronting armed posses of sheriffs' deputies, Ku Klux Klan etc. (Backcloth 7.)

Enter BOSSES: *followed by* IMMIGRANT WORKERS, *who start building furiously.*

1st Boss We're gonna build, we're gonna build,
    We're gonna build these United States – –
2nd Boss We are in business, we're gonna build,
    We're gonna scrape the skies with steel and concrete – –
3rd Boss We're gonna build, we are in business, the whole New World is
    filled
    With the need and the desire to climb higher higher higher
    Till we walk the highest wire – –
1st Boss The highest wire the longest drop:
    Yet at all times at the top
    There will be one man standing tall –
Bosses And he stands there for us all!
1st Boss So let's get moving. Hustle. We got construction to complete. We got millions and millions of free citizens to complete it for us: and Jesus Christ we gotta deadline!
3rd Boss So let's look at what we got. We got Irish, we got Eyetalians, we got Polacks, we got Swedes – so according to their ethnic categories, let's arrange them into gangs – and for each gang we give a flag, and the first gang to hit the roof, the flag of their national origin flies over the completed structure! Say, how's about that for an incentive – come on – you *dummkopf* immigrants – move!

Improvised race between groups of workers to see which group builds to the top first. The winners greeted with enthusiasm and their flag raised. Songs of different nations sung all together: and the workers disperse exuberantly. Enter GOMPERS. (*During this scene he is constantly distracted by the telephone, he answers briefly, issuing instructions for strikes etc . . . business to be improvised.*)

Gompers (*to audience*) Hi. Say, folks, you know me – warm-hearted, generous-natured, cordial-spirited Sam Gompers, the very essence of the schmaltzy sympathy that puts America where it is! Do you want I should level with you, do you want I should ingratiatingly make the flesh on your backbone creep? Okay: I'll give it you straight. As of right now, nineteen hundred and three, I am constitutional president of the American Federation of Labor – a trade union organiser is all – elected thereto December eighteen hundred and eighty-six having heretofore presided over the New York branch of the Cigar Makers' Union, having heretofore made cigars, in a Lower East Side sweatshop at the age of thirteen. The New World, the golden pavements, my friends, you should be so lucky! Like I told you, I pack wallop. Like I told you, the American bosses don't like my name one little bit: yet with them I can sing and dance, yeah, with these guys I can go places . . . Hey, folks, just watch 'em sweat!

Sings:

> My name is Samuel Gompers and the American labour movement
> Depends on me for all its huge advancement and improvement.

If they don't accept me then who do they accept? Saboteurs, agitators, God knows what from God knows where – let 'em figger it out and hear them settle for the roach on the kitchen floor – yeah, sure they'd rather that than a tribe of alligators in the drains.

Bosses (*sing*)
> Gompers is the boy for us, Gompers knows his onions,
> We all rely on Gompers for responsible trade unions.

Gompers (*sings*)
> If the bosses all will undertake to recognise my outfit –

Bosses The AF of L. . . .

Gompers (*sings*) I promise in return that I –

So make it sweet for 'em, why not? Pat their backs to burp their pap up –

> I promise in return that I will never hog the market.

So let's have some lousy give-and-take around here: gentlemen, state your needs.

Bosses (*sing*)
> We must have immigrants and blacks and dirty yellow dagoes
> To hire and fire at our own desire and moderate the payroll.

Gompers (*sings*)
> And Irishmen and Eyeties too – I keep 'em where you need 'em:
> I never question what you pay or how you choose to bleed 'em.
> I keep 'em out and keep well in the loyal white-skinned Yankee
> Whom I so firmly organise, there'll be no hanky-panky!
> No wildcat strikes, no lockings-out, discreet negotiations
> Ensure your peace and quiet to build –

Bosses (*sing*)
>Cartels and combinations.
>Wages rise but prices fall, production costs are stable –
>Sam Gompers does his work for us as long as he is able.
>United Steel, the Railroad Trust, the House of Rockefeller,
>All join together hand-in-hand to fill the nation's cellar:
>A chicken hot in every pot, good news for every organ –
>And don't forget the enormous debt we owe to Pierpoint
>>Morgan . . .!

Enter GRABITALL (*as J. P. Morgan*), *and takes a bow as the* BOSSES *dance a brief reprise.*

Grabitall Who controls through interlocking directorates no less than one quarter of the nation's total corporate assets! Gentlemen, lift your hats!

They all lift their hats and stand for a few seconds in silence.

Mr Gompers, in my opinion, associations of working men in restraint of lawful trade are repugnant to the constitution.

Gompers Mr Grabitall, your great trading enterprises depend on purchase of raw materials in the best possible market. So the working men you hire to process those raw materials are a raw material themselves: and they have left it up to me to determine their own market. The skill of a trained craft worker is a commodity he puts a price on: you meet the man's price, you're entitled to the merchandise. If not – –

Grabitall In the market where I deal I fix my own prices.

Gompers So we strike you and we picket you and you lock us out, why not, and then there ain't no market on God's earth for you to deal in! So what do you do then? Look, in eighteen ninety-three in the AF of L, an attempt is made already to commit the outfit to a socialist platform: we defeated that attempt. Do you want we should be so alienated our rank-and-file would try it again?

Grabitall You'd have me believe that to recognise trade unions will consolidate private enterprise?

Gompers You'd better believe it. Mister, I don't want no more than what you want: – *more: here: now!* In a free market! So meet those terms.

Sings:
>Sure we came here to make it
>We came here to make it
>We came here to make it
>To make it to the top!

Grabitall (*sings*)
>If I don't cut your throat
>If I don't cut your throat
>If I don't cut your throat
>Then my throat's gonna be cut!

Bosses (*sing*)

> So I jump on your back
> So you jump on my back
> And I jump on your back
> We're all of us gonna be rich!

Gompers

> We call it pioneering
> We call it high-frontiering]
> We call it buccanneering
> Watch me slay the son-of-a-bitch!

His telephone rings.

Yeah, Gompers here, AF of L . . . yeah . . . yeah . . . so leave it with me, I'll fix it, in the meantime tell your membership you have strike-action authorised as from Monday week.

He rings off.

That's the boilermakers' local from the Roanoke shops of the West Virginia Railroad: seems like we have a problem. Rate for the job in accordance with our agreement of June nineteen hundred and two should be as from five dollars on a pro-rata basis – management there sticks hard at four dollars fifty. Demand must be met by seven days next Monday or we yank them boilermakers out. Okay, next business?

His phone is ringing again and he picks it up and answers it. Other phones ring and BOSSES *answer them.*

1st Boss We gotta problem. There's a pile-up of stocks of winter coal in the Blue Valley Mining Company's yards has gotta be shifted by October or production comes to a standstill. And without we have in action the new locomotives – –

2nd Boss That Blue Valley coal is on order to Consolidated Edison Electric Power, New York, demand for installation of new street lighting in East Brooklyn, if not met, threatens breach of contract with city authorities. We gotta problem.

3rd Boss We got more than a problem, we gotta goddam catastrophe. There's an Attorney General's Investigatory Board looking into the New York electrical contracts division right now: and all they want to clinch their case is evidence of kickbacks on the overall Con-Ed dealings. It could affect the election!

Bosses It could affect the election, it could affect the election, it could affect the election!!

Grabitall How's the share index?

1st Boss West Virginia Railroad, down down down.

2nd Boss Consolidated Edison, down down down . . .

Grabitall Gompers, you gotta *act*!! Them West Virginian locomotives has gotta be rolling by – –

Gompers Monday week? Five dollars. Tell you what, boss, make it easy. Call it four seventy-three and hold over the twenty-seven.

Grabitall Hold it over until when?

Gompers Till finalised formulation of an advanced agreement next year. Retrospective, with inflation, sure, you'll bleed, but you'll never know it.

Grabitall Four-seventy.

Gompers Seventy-three.

Grabitall Seventy-three . . .

Gompers I'll tell the boys . . . (*On the telephone*) Hello, Roanoke? We had an answer. Four dollars seventy-three. That's ten cents a man more than you asked me to hang out for. Yeah, sure, we're doing business . . .

Grabitall (*to* BOSSES) I want them blueprints. Now look here, you see these, there's an expert assessment here of a total re-run of the Roanoke shop-layout – conveyor belts, mass production, every part of the locomotive fixed into position by one man after another who need no special skill beyond the elemental ability to slot a peg into a hole as the fabric is rolled in front of 'em. Replace fifty bone-idle boilermakers with three hundred Polack woodchoppers who never saw a steam engine in their lives before, production of locomotives goes up five hundred per cent, the payroll is cut by sixty per cent, and the grip of the goddam union is shaken off for for ever. Don't you see, there ain't no stopping us!

They run out cheering.

Gompers So don't think I don't know what these guys are cooking up for me. The logical conclusion of industrial mass production is the mass-basis industrial union. I'm allergic. My unions are of craftsmen to protect only their own craft, because, tell me, what does a man honour more than the skill of his own hands? What else does he have that should make him a man? Let them bring in their conveyor belts. Five hundred Polack woodchoppers – oh I read that bastard's mind but good – but between 'em they'll produce no boilers unless there's one boilermaker on the job to tell 'em how to do it. And by me that guy's protected! I yank him outa the plant: the entire line runs into the ground. That one guy, an *employee*, is the king of his production-line: pumpkin-pie and kraut-and-wieners his goddam bosses'll have to feed him if they want to keep him crowned for them. And Sam Gompers sees they do. That one guy, in an AF of L Union, keeps all four hundred and forty-nine alongside of him in employment – in good wages – so for what do they need a union? It's logical, it's practical, it's American, it's democratic – –

He sings:

> I really cannot understand how anyone can imagine
> How anything is wrong at all with such a useful system?

Yet here they are, the theorists, the left-wing agitators,
Who do their best from east to west to undermine my status!

SCENE 2

Enter DEBS *and* DE LEON, *with placards indicative of their respective parties.*

Gompers Socialism . . . ! Thank God there's two of 'em. Thank God they don't agree. Thank God they hate each other's guts. Eugene Debs – the Socialist Party of America – rabble-rousers and roused rabble, cornfed mid-west revivalism mixed in with smoking axle-grease! Here's a slob that believed all the slobs should go together, an industrial union of every man in the railroad industry no less – 'cepting of course the niggers, not even Debs got room for them – forms his own national union, cuts right across the separate trades in the AF of L, and pulls 'em all out on strike in eighteen hundred and ninety-four: for a general national wage-hike for every railroadman in the land? Get wise. They struck in *sympathy*: for the men who built the Pullman cars their hearts bled and they struck. And they *were* struck – weren't they, Debs? The US Army, horse and foot, came down on Chicago like the locusts came on Egypt –

Debs Yes sir, that strike was broke. And we would not have been broke had the AF of L at the moment of need stood fast by our right hand and – –

Gompers Debs, don't talk to me. Go talk to Dan De Leon.

De Leon Why send him to talk to me? He talked to me often before, he could have learned his lesson before. He could have learned his lesson from me that Sam Gompers is no lost soul to be driven to remorse and penitence by appealing to his past transgressions: but a live and active enemy of the American working class: who deliberately set out to destroy the Railway Union in alliance with the federal army.

Gompers What he means, folks, is just this, that his Socialist Labor Party exists for one purpose – to establish a set of unions devoted to alien ideology and subvert the American working man from his natural way of life.

De Leon *My* unions, the Associated Trade and Labor Alliance, are informed at all stages by the scientific doctrine of the properly-constituted political party, measured and tested against the yardstick of informed international socialist opinion.

Gompers For *your* party, Eugene Debs, they got no better word than a pack of kangaroos.

De Leon *My* phrase, Brother Gompers –

Gompers Why not mine? They jump here, they jump there, among the AFL, among the Democrats, among the nigra-hating rednecks of the Deep South even: Debs, go take a jump right outta my yard!

De Leon And consider, Debs, before you do, just who is going to give the orders to the United States Cavalry the next time you jump so high.

Debs The only ones who should ever give orders to the United States Cavalry are the people of the United States for the furtherance and defence of their democratic rights. I am for socialism because I am for humanity. The time has come to regenerate society – I believe we are on the eve of a universal change! Comrade De Leon: so long as your Associated Trade and Labor Alliance remains unable to extend its membership beyond the bounds of last week's shipment of bigoted Silesian sectarian conspirators, you will stay as you ever have been, way outside the mainstream of the drive of this great nation towards the promised land of social justice!

Exit.

Gompers Yeah . . . he said the mainstream. Come on, Dan, tell the world that you and only you can diagnose the course of *all* streams, main and tributary.

De Leon The mainstream, of course, is the Socialist Labor Party because only the Socialist Labor Party is directly the product of the American section of the First Socialist International. I won't waste words on Gompers. In due course the development of the Associated Trade and Labor Alliance will overtake and break his collaborationist union-structure. As for Debs, he talks big: and his party membership is no doubt big. But do you know I don't believe you could find one single member of that opportunist organisation to talk the same way he talks? Thousands and thousands of dedicated worthy souls: the tower of Babel will be their monument. Now in *my* party, there is discipline, lectures, discussions, correctly-organised public activity: and the central organ of the party, my newspaper, *The Weekly People*, is the corner-stone of that activity.

Gompers (*singing*)

> Yeah, newspapers, any mug can read and write
> Let anyone who wants to, set his notions up in type.
> But it ain't no editorials of resounding high desire
> In the end will fire the flame upon the pyramids of power –
> No, Sam Gompers has a trickier way to go:
> When the working class knows nuth'n, boys, there's nuth'n for
> them to know –

Know-nuth'n's where they were, know-nuth'n is where they will be, even *after* they read my newspaper: so to find out who they are, who to tell them but Sam Gompers? – Sam Gompers indispensable, Sam Gompers can never be toppled. Watch it.

Exit GOMPERS.

SCENE 3

De Leon We cannot afford to have the revolution conducted by amateurs. Where is Mr Lyon?

The full bustle of a newspaper office surrounds him, people passing papers, delivering proofs, dictating memos etc. The MANAGER *comes for orders.*

Frank, I want an article on the front page, if you please, condemning yet again the tendency of those ex-party members who split away from us in ninety-nine and allied themselves with Eugene Debs.

Manager Mr De Leon, you said all that in your article last month –

De Leon It has to be said again, Frank, if only to convince our readership that the retrograde anti-party internal conspiracy of eighteen ninety-nine is still alive in Debs's ranks and seeks every possible opportunity of re-infiltrating the SLP!

Manager Yessir, Mr De Leon, will you write it yourself?

De Leon Of course, I'll go right in, set to work on it now.

Manager Rabinovitch! Goddammit, man, will you hold the front page – Mr De Leon has decided to write a new leading article . . .

The general bustle of the office continues. DE LEON *retires.* CONNOLLY *enters, with his emigrant's luggage.*

Connolly (*sings*)

> With a song upon me lips and a pack upon me back
> I have travelled o'er the ocean upon me weary track.
> From the coast of Erin's isle to the harbour of New York
> Rambling Pat across the world comes looking out for work!

(*speaks*)

> And both me eyes opened wide with a round regard for
>   opportunity
> I fetch the ferrule of me wee stick to the Socialist Labor Party!
> Not of course for the first time I've been in front of this door:
> Indeed, to tell the truth of it, I was here just last year.
> And every year there are men leave Ireland by the thousand and
>   the thousand score.
> Driven out by their landlords, driven out by the police,
> Driven out very simply only because they are so poor
> Sure it's easy enough to tell that I too at the root of it am but one
>   of these:
> I wonder could you also tell that in my case there is something
>   more . . . ?

For am I not the man who created in Dublin the Irish Socialist Republican Party; devised, edited and personally sold the party newspaper *The Workers' Republic*; and in the year nineteen hundred sent no less than two delegates to the International Socialist Congress at Paris – and all this upon the quivering bog-rotten resources of the pre-industrial Irish peasant economy – what can I not do for the movement in *this* country – what can I not do in this newspaper? Hardly a job in these offices I will not be able to fill! And for party-work at last within a truly well-organised group – oh the ugly duckling indeed has left his puddle and found blue water! Hello – Frank . . . !

Manager (*rushes past and bumps into* CONNOLLY) What the hell are you doin' here, mac! You're in the way, get outta the way, we gotta deadline to beat!

Connolly But Frank, Frank Lyon, you know me –

Manager (*talks across* CONNOLLY's *stammer*) Say, do I know you? Why, sure, Jim Connolly – Jim Connolly from Dublin, Ireland. Am I right? Glad to see ya again, Jim, how long will ya be in New York, say we oughta meet up some time, have a drink, swop some yarns, I got business just this moment . . .

Connolly Look, Frank: I want a job. I've come back to New York on a – yes, well – on a permanent basis. D'you suppose you could find me –

Manager Job? What sorta job? Oh no, Rabinovitch, no – willya tell the cartoonist Pierpoint Morgan as an octopus was in Debs's paper last week – the Kangaroos of the SPA are the assignment he was given – Godsake, he's a goddam artist, let him show some creativity!

Connolly I am a qualified linotype operative, Heriot Watt College, Edinburgh, and I hoped – –

Manager You're a qualified whatsit? Say, we printed the posters for your lectures last year, you were billed as an unskilled labourer: what gives, boy, you trying to con me?

Connolly Between last year and this I have qualified as a – –

Manager Okay so you qualified. You gotta union card?

Connolly Naturally not yet, but I've no doubt I could – –

Manager AF of L closed shop in this business. No union card, no job.

Gompers (*re-enters briefly*) That's right, that's how it goes . . . yeah . . .

Connolly I see. Would there be perhaps a chance in the editorial department?

Manager You wanna write for the paper? Go talk to Dan De Leon – Christ, I only *produce* his goddam organ, what else? – will ya do me a favour, will ya let these presses roll? Rabinovitch, I want them proof-sheets!

Exit MANAGER. CONNOLLY, *disconsolate, goes towards* DE LEON *who is at his desk, writing.*

De Leon Comrade Connolly, well, well, well, this is a surprise. Oh you have all your baggage, I see, maybe not after all so much of a surprise. I didn't imagine it would be long possible for a young man of your ambition to rusticate in Dublin, Ireland. So you have come around at last to the correct point of view. The New World, comrade, the massive industry, the teeming population, the ferment of constant social mobility – only here can mankind after centuries lay hold of his ultimate noble destiny. You will settle in New York?

Connolly I was enquiring about a job on *The Weekly People* . . . as a linotype operator, but . . .

De Leon Ah – you should see my manager about that. Frank Lyon, I think you know him – ?

Connolly Yes. Er – on the editorial department –

De Leon Well, naturally, any article you care to write upon political or economic matters will be seriously considered for publication in the newspaper. But you will first of course have applied for membership of your local branch of the SLP, and then anything you put your pen to can be checked out with the membership there before you submit it: and errors of political emphasis eliminated and corrected. I wonder what will be your local branch . . . where are you staying?

Connolly (*very cast down*) I . . . er . . . I imagine, to begin with, I won't actually be in New York. I have cousins up the Hudson River, in the town of Troy, I can stay with them.

De Leon Troy. Yes indeed, we have a flourishing branch in Troy. Let me know how you get on there – I'm sure that in a year or two we shall be hearing your name quite frequently in the reports of our party activities . . .

Connolly (*almost with violence*) Comrade De Leon, I do think I am capable, you know, of being very useful to you on this newspaper!

De Leon Comrade Connolly, we need men who have thoroughly mastered the essential idea of the identity of America, and the leading place this country holds in the future of world socialism. You can get that in Troy quite as well as anywhere else.

Connolly But when I was here last year –

De Leon You lectured for me very competently upon conditions in Ireland. Yes. And it was certainly of advantage for us to show the American-Irish that an unskilled Dublin labourer could be as keenly imbued as any night-school graduate with the elements of scientific socialism. But now you are settled here for good, as you tell me, the task before you is – –

Connolly Can I scotch once and for all this unskilled labourer business. I have been a professional political organiser since eighteen hundred and ninety-six, and –

De Leon Didn't I hear you say something about linotype-operating? Are we not a little inconsistent?

Connolly Comrade De Leon, is not your manager maybe not a little inconsistent? He told me I would need a union card from the AF of L.

De Leon Correct.

Connolly You recognise the AF of L? But in the meantime your own trade union – –

De Leon The Associated Trade and Labor Alliance. Yes.

Connolly You tell me it is not recognised in your own publishing house, Comrade De Leon!

De Leon Are we to close down because Brother Gompers blacks our product? Is our analytical voice throughout the land to be muffled because an enthusiastic young man from a pre-industrial economy prefers impracticable idealism to the hard struggle of political tactic? Enough of this foolishness, my good friend: go to Troy: learn your business.

CONNOLLY *makes as though to go.*

Oh comrade, just one moment. The Irish Socialist Republican Party has collapsed in disorder, has it not, despite all your professional organising since eighteen ninety-six?

Connolly There were reasons for that collapse. We have no more than the very beginnings of a revolutionary proletariat – we – –

De Leon You were requested to resign after a premature attempt to enter local electoral politics. I suspect you have a tendency to be premature in many matters. The secretary of the Troy Branch of the Socialist Labor Party, Comrade Passano, is a very careful man and very precise as to his theory. When you get to know him I suggest you follow his example as accurately as you can. Good morning, comrade. Glad to have met you again.

Exit DE LEON.

SCENE 4

The stage fills with children running backwards and forwards with parcels of linen products – an urgent chorus of 'Collars and cuffs, dollars and cents, cents and dollars, cuffs and collars, call it Troy, call it Arrow, call it Arrow, call it shirt . . .'

Connolly Troy. My cousins are glad to see me: they go so far as find a house for me to rent so my wife and my six children can come over from Ireland just as soon as I'm settled. So how do I get settled? I told them I would be working for De Leon's paper, and I'm not. I need an opening for a man with no recognisable skill: but a certain facility at putting people's backs up . . . door-to-door commission work, the all-American answer . . . the Metropolitan Life Insurance Company: here they are.

Enter insurance company MANAGER.

I want a job.

Manager Experience?

Connolly No. I was for a while a class of a pedlar in Dublin . . .

Manager No experience. So what? You're a human being. What better experience can you have? So here's a list of our customers between Tenth Street and Twenty-fifth, they pay twenty cents a week for accident/ disability/funeral insurance: and it's up to you to collect it. You get seven cents for every dollar you pull in. If you want to increase your commission, you increase your list of customers. How you do it is your business. But if they don't pay, you don't get paid: get it? Okay.

Connolly Well, here I am on Eleventh Street: I suppose these are all my customers.

Manager So right away get into it. Disintegrate the competition. Get your
percentage off the ground.

Connolly It's not very promising. Who are all these wee children tearing back
and forwards with parcels of linen? Is there a first communion, or
what – ?

Manager Company runners for the Arrow shirt factory. It's a company town
this. Call it Troy, call it Arrow, call it Arrow, call it shirt –

Connolly Call it shirt, call it sweatshop . . .

Manager Call it what? It's good business. Why friend, there's hardly a
human being in this town over the age of five unemployed. It's the other
side of Main Street you get the bad influence.

Connolly Eh?

Manager An outfit of socialists in a boarded-up store front. Beats me the cops
haven't raided the joint. Keep a tight hold on your bankroll if you find
yourself in that area. Okay, friend, get to it. . . .

Exit.

Connolly So the boarded-up store front was the first place I went.

> I was known to the SLP here. My reputation a little bent,
> I discovered, by my being Irish. Dan De Leon, it appeared,
> Had conveyed a general aroma that all born catholics were men
>   to be feared:
> And the work in the party that they gave me was in accordance
>   somewhat slow.
> Quite a contrast with the speed at which my two feet had to go
> In frantic search for the daily dollars for the Metropolitan Life
> And my own meagre seven per cent for myself and my house and
>   my wife . . .
> My list is long and I am not strong
> And I cannot but think there is something very wrong
> When twenty cents a week to ensure a poor man his grave
> Cuts the heart out of his body even while he is still alive.

So let's have a look at it. Number three five three eight Fifteenth Street,
here we are, overflowing dustbins on the steps of the porch, overflowing
children in and out of the dustbins, a dog, goddammit – get out of it –
ow! Ah you wouldn't ever think I'd ever left Dublin. Oh these staircases.
Knock knock. He's not on my list: but I'll give him a try. Good morning,
sir, I represent the Metropolitan Life – I wonder if I could induce you
to buy some insurance . . .

Customer And I wonder if I could induce you, Comrade Connolly, to take
some of these copies of *The Weekly People* on your rounds?

Connolly If I'd known it was you, comrade, I wouldn't have bothered you. If
you want any insurance, sure you can get it from me at the party offices.
In fact I do sell the newspaper to half-a-dozen of my customers: if I
need more I'll let you know.

Customer Tell me, the insurance business: is good these days: or slow?

Connolly Slow.

Customer I think slower than the production at the shirt factory, yes? Did you hear, they have this speed-up?

Connolly Heavy?

Customer Is two hundredweight extra work for every operative: no wage increase. There is talk even of a strike. Now here is a question of interest for both of us. I am a member of the AF of L shirt-makers' local. Have to be, is all there is! Is either now strike or lockout, I don't know which. What now will be done by our Socialist Labor Party?

Connolly Did you talk to Passano about it?

Customer Ach, Passano. All he says is: 'What for the hell you in an AFL union, comrade? The party has its own union.' I tell him, 'Not in Troy, not the Arrow plant, so what to do?' I tell him, 'Give me literature from the party in support of this strike, I will distribute in our local, maybe the strike or lockout will then from the start become a move towards socialism, revolution: solidarity!' He tell me nonsense.

Connolly Nonsense? What do you mean, nonsense?

Customer He tell me to demand better wages for increased production is no more than to put up prices so we are all where we were before. If the union call a strike, then I too must go on strike, but I must not trouble myself to instigate such action, no: nor yet expect the party to concern itself in any way. I ask you, Comrade Connolly, do you consider this good sense?

Connolly Dear God, this is worse than nonsense. Did he justify it?

Customer Passano? He said: is correct doctrine. He said to read weekly *The Weekly People*. I said not only do I read but I sell the damned paper. Where, I said, in all this paper do you find it is good socialism to keep the proletariat ignorant of the strength of their own struggle? *Teufelsdreck*, is a branch secretary, tells me nothing but nonsense.

Connolly We could bring it up at the branch meeting, I suppose. But Passano will – –

Customer Will fuck about with his agenda: it will never be discussed. Now I am not so good with the English, *nicht wahr*? But for you, you could do it, you could write –

Connolly I could write to the paper and have the whole thing put out in public. Why wouldn't I? I will –

Exeunt.

SCENE 5

Enter GOMPERS.

Gompers Sure a letter to the party, what harm can a man do?
United we rise, divided we fall, that's all –

If you hadn'ta wanted to splash your vest, you shouldn'ta pissed so close to the wall!

Exit GOMPERS. *Enter* DE LEON *with a letter: and his newspaper* MANAGER.

De Leon The single-handed creation out of nothing of the foremost revolutionary party in this great country, of the only revolutionary party in this entire hemisphere: first the master, then the disciples, then the completely informed and corrected nucleus of activists and agitators: and finally, the masses, in control of their own destiny. There is a flaw in it, what's the flaw? I will tell you: the very make-up of the masses themselves upon the moment of their arrival: they unwittingly succumb to the anarchic laissez-faire of the American way of life, within the very context of the socialist theory itself. Comrade Connolly has taken it upon himself to write this letter to *The Weekly People.* He criticises the official stance of the Socialist Labor Party upon wages, upon unionisation, upon marriage, upon religion, upon God knows what. I have asked the secretayy of the Troy branch of the party to call in and have a word about it next time he was in New York. In the meanwhile, Frank, we will publish this letter – without amendment. It does come from a paid-up member: and by open controversy alone can such gross errors be corrected. Go see if Passano's here . . . Fragmentism, economicism: this fool could split the party just like it was split before! My God I thought we'd cleaned that mess for good and all . . .

MANAGER *goes off and brings in* PASSANO.

Comrade Passano. Very glad you could find the time. Did Comrade Connolly tell you he was preparing this effusion?

Passano No, comrade De Leon, he didn't . . . So what do we do with him? Expel him?

De Leon Dear me, no: no no no. We must make a strong attempt to put him back on the right path.

Passano Sure, sure, I do appreciate he challenges the very leadership of the party with his – –

De Leon Not so much the leadership – the entire *structure* he calls in question! From his experience of the potato-trade in Ireland, he comes over here to lecture us! Of course he's out for nothing but his own personal publicity. Do you hear how he concludes his letter? 'I hold that mine is the correct SLP doctrine. Now will someone please tread on the tail of my coat!'

Manager The son-of-a-bitch is flippant.

De Leon But self-assertive. Oh yes. Comrade Passano: you make sure you keep your eye on him in your branch. The letter in the newspaper will be taken care of in the newspaper.

Passano Yessir, Mr De Leon, thank you, sir: I'll do just that. . . .

Exit PASSANO.

De Leon Tread on the tail of his coat . . . ! Oh yes, what he asks for, he will certainly get. But upon our terms, not his.

Exeunt.

SCENE 6

Enter CONNOLLY, *some Troy* SLP MEMBERS, *some* WORKING WOMEN.

Connolly If we're not going to do anything, then nothing will be done. My opinion, it's high time we stopped confounding ourselves with theory and took a long strong look at what's happening in this town.

1st Member (*Connolly's customer from Scene 4*) I ask please for you comrades to take your noses from *The Weekly People*: we have a branch meeting in ten minutes and the agenda is about what? About speed-up, about strike? About the shirt-collar trust conspiracy that puts all Troy upon the bread-line? If not, I say why not?

2nd Member Don't yell at me. There's one helluva shellacking right on the front page from Comrade De Leon about that damnfool letter you wrote – Connolly, I'm talking to you! You out to make the name of the Troy branch stink from one end of the party to the other – or what –

Connolly Comrade, these young ladies here have *not* read *The Weekly People*: they have come to our committee-rooms to interest a united and intelligent group of political activists in *their* problem, their problem alone. Do we do them the courtesy to give them our full attention? Ladies?

Woman Worker (*with interjections and prompting from her friends*) Look, we ain't in no trade union: and we don't know about no politics. We're all from the Bluett-Peabody plant –

Connolly Subsidiary of Arrow Shirts, right?

Woman Worker We make the collars, see, starched collars: they put in this new starcher, works off a gasoline engine, starching and pressing like on a – like on a cable-railway, sorta . . .

1st Member Conveyor-belt technique: creates the redundancy of one-third of the women hand-starchers.

Woman Worker But this machine it don't work so good. So they cut piece-work rates by half, speed up the whole shop, give us overtime without the option: and any work on the machine that they say comes through spoiled – –

1st Member *Mein Gott* with that machine, is *all* of it spoiled!

Woman Worker If it's spoiled they take the cost of it out of our pay. And if any of us falls down for one minute on the job – –

1st Member The sister of my wife Truda herself for sneezing at her work is all, has dismissal given her yesterday! As I inform you, conspiracy: Bluett-Peabody, *mit* Arrow, *mit* one two three *vier fünf* six *sieben* – is nine altogether *fabriken* in Troy *zusammen kaput*!

3rd Member Okay okay, hold it, Hans, you're after leaving us all behind . . .

Woman Worker He means we've walked out – in nine factories, we've all walked out. We're on strike.

Connolly Deliberate pressure by nine companies to *force* them all out on strike – sure they know the AF of L has only a minute fraction of the Troy workforce properly organised: and they mean to break all hope of any further unionisation in this industry from now on! I suppose you have your demands worked out?

Woman Worker Sure thing, mister, we've worked 'em out! Say, take a look at this!

She hands CONNOLLY *a paper.*

Connolly I see. Very good indeed. And now you deserve and need the very fullest political support that the committed socialist movement can give you – and not only in Troy – now here, comrades, is surely something that the SLP with its press facilities can – –

Enter PASSANO *and some more* SLP MEMBERS.

Passano What the hell goes on round here? We gotta branch meeting, not a social. Will you get these broads outta here pronto? Don't you know that the meetings is exclusive to the membership?

1ST MEMBER *whispers in his ear.*

Oh . . . Oh yeah . . . Comrade Connolly . . . ? It figgers . . . Look, ladies, I guess there's some mistake, this ain't no meeting yet to discuss your dispute. Say, we'll take a report from the member that brought you in here, and when maybe we've considered it, there'll be some sort of action forthcoming, I can't say what. Sure we know where to get in touch with you, we'll let you know, okay, good-night . . . So let's have some order around here, this is a meeting!

Exeunt WOMEN, *dissatisfied.*

1st Member Now look, comrade: first things first. Important beyond all things we give help to the people in Troy.

3rd Member I think maybe there's a good case here for an immediate resolution. Sure to God those girls have spirit. If we don't stand up with 'em, they'll be left to the AF of L. . .

Passano First things first? On *my* agenda first things first is Comrade Connolly and his indiscipline – has he or has he not been attacking the party in public! If he has, he should be punished. But seems it ain't to be up to us to decide whether he has or he hasn't. I gotta communication here from Comrade De Leon, no less. He says, don't mess with it in Troy. Now it's ventilated in *The Weekly People*, the place to discuss it, what he calls the 'appropriate forum' is the national convention, to be held in six weeks.

Connolly And in the meantime – –

Passano In the meantime how far do you comrades want to debate the attitude to Comrade Connolly we should adopt at this convention?

1st Member Debate? Debate nothing! Circulate such debates among the wage-slaves of New York State in order to make them more prejudiced against us? Comrades, *Gott in Himmel*, be as cunning and as cute as the capitalists are: but *Sakrament*, do not confuse the true and only purpose of the struggle of the working class!

Loud expressions of approval, and disapproval for PASSANO.

Passano Okay okay okay – discussion on this matter adjourned *sine die*. So we leave it to the convention. Comrade Connolly – you'd better be there.

Exeunt all but CONNOLLY (*one or two clap him on the back as they leave*), *and* 3RD MEMBER, *who is Irish*.

Connolly There's a hell of a lot of work to be done. All those out on strike who aren't in the union need strike funds collected for them. Sure, I can do some of it on my insurance-company rounds – if it comes to that, those out on strike who aren't in the union are finding so much difficulty in paying their insurance, I guess it leaves me with all the time in the world. Collect funds, sell the newspaper – ugh, with my name mud in it – get out a few hand-duplicated leaflets of my own – Passano's a dead loss, the party-branch as a branch does nothing: but we have friends . . . most of them, as it happens from the Irish quarter . . .

3rd Member No comment . . .

Enter insurance MANAGER.

Manager Hey, Connolly, I want you! Look, feller, the assets of this office as of right now are frozen. So hand over your books, and your current takings – if any.

Connolly You mean – –

Manager I mean you're fired. In this situation, with half of Troy out of work, there just ain't no future here in the insurance business.

Connolly But who's to collect the subscriptions from now on?

Manager You deaf or sum'pn – no-one!

Connolly But some of these people have been paying you money for years . . .

Manager If they'd wanted to continue to be covered by our policies, they oughta had more sense than to be agitated into a strike! And who by? Don't tell me! I'm wise to you, Connolly! The Metropolitan Life Insurance Company tucks its shingle under its arm and takes the first train outta town!

Exit MANAGER.

Connolly There are times when I wonder whether
        The old practice of tar-and-feather
        Would not have its good uses elsewhere than the Far West . . .

> And any time now my family comes from Ireland – oh God,
> what to do for the best . . . ?

3rd Member Jim, get out of Troy as soon as you can, find work where you can get it, feed your stomach for the fight – you've stirred up enough of us here to carry on where you've left off.

Exeunt.

SCENE 7

Enter HAYWOOD.* MINERS *with placards ('Western Federation of Miners on strike for 8-hour day') stand behind him. They all have pistols or rifles.*

Haywood (*sings*)

> Way out west there's a union built, and we built it strong and
> wild:
> The Western Federation of Miners, Goliath the giant's child,
> We got no truck with tenderfoot pussyfoots, if we're beaten we
> never will yield,
> In the town of Leadville Colorado for a year we have held the
> field –
> For a year and a day so take it away
> Big Bill Haywood is my name
> Revolution is my aim
> . . . So take it away . . .

You'd better get this and get it good, across the prairie into the mountains there ain't never no end to a strike but gunfire and bloodshed: yeah they call in the yellow-leg horse-soldiers and they shoot us down in the streets like dogs . . .

> In the town of Leadville Colorado we been striking for the eight-
> hour day
> We'll never sit down to starve to death but fight it every yard of
> the way
> Let 'em shoot us dead and harry us in to the bull-pen or the
> county jail
> I tell it to you and I tell it true our courage will never fail:
> A year and a day so take it away
> Big Bill Haywood is my name
> Revolution is my aim
> . . . So take it away . . .

> And take away too your AF of L setting slave against jealous
> slave:

* Haywood is a one-eyed man.

United miners stand or fall into many a lonely grave
In Salt Lake City, Coeur d'Alene, Telluride and Cripple Creek
When the bosses and the bulls come hunting blood they don't
    have far to seek:
A year and a day so take it away
Big Bill Haywood is my name
Revolution is my aim
. . . So take it away . . .

Ain't no doubt about it, the men of the West has the Easterners licked
for militance, endurance, revolutionary sure-fire grit: class-conscious?
We got noth'n in these mountains to live on but pit-props, and boy,
that's a diet sure will stiffen a man's neck!

A fair day's wage for a fair day's work? Trash, boy, take it away!
Abolition of the whole wage-system is the only game we play:
Abolition of the American boss-class, destruction of the power
    of gold:
And who's gonna help us grab this nation from the plutocratic
    hold?
For a year and a day so take it away
If we get no help we'll die where we stand
With gun in hand
. . . So take it away . . . !

1st Miner

From the coalfields of Illinois here comes old Mother Jones
To lend us the strength of her seventy-five-year-old bones.

Enter MOTHER JONES.

Mother Jones

Eugene Debs of the SPA
Is coming to help you, to help you today!
He's a-coming to Leadville on the high-noon train
To set this union on its feet again!

Haywood

Boys, give a welcome to Eugene Debs with your pistols at your
    hip –
If the Pinkerton finks and the company bulls hear that man shoot
    off his lip
There ain't no insurance outfit take a policy on Debs's life:
The dark dark nights of Colorado make a widow of a socialist
    wife!

2nd Miner

Here comes his train, hear the engine blow and blow –

1st Miner

> What way will the sheriff and his deputy-killers sneak around and
> try to go . . . ?

Sound of train arriving. DEBS *enters, and is immediately guarded by the*
MINERS *as armed labour detectives lurk in the shadows.*

1st Detective

> Now lookit, boys, go careful, don't try nuth'n sudden and rough:
> Bill Haywood and his gunmen radicals are out today to play it
> tough –

2nd Detective

> Bill Haywood and his gutless gunmen are bringing in too many
> friends –

1st Detective

> High time this subversive anti-American conspiracy was brought
> to an end.
> Socialist leaders outta the East, next time it'll be a Democrat!
> We gotta find a way the shit leaks outta the brim of Bill
> Haywood's hat,
> Find a way the radical bastard's face is streaked with worse than
> tears –
> Put him away, put him away for years.

2nd Detective

> Like for murder . . . who's he killed?

1st Detective

> No-one yet, but he will . . .

The DETECTIVES *sneak back into the wings.*

Haywood Look, Gene, this miners' union gets nowhere because we've got no
ties with the rest of the national working class: the rest of the national
working class are stifled and bound by the swaddling clothes of Sam
Gompers. From coast to coast there are millions of men outside of the
corral of the AFL who want to organise but find no framework.

Debs I've come to Colorado specific to discuss just such a framework. For
the lack of it in ninety-four, the Pullman strike, we were drowned down.
I have a list here of thirty names, all of them in some way leaders of
radical groups.

Haywood That's it, that's what we want. Now if you, me, and Mother Jones
was to get them guys together, in secret to begin with, and then talk them
all together, and by God *hold* them together –

Mother Jones Hold a wildcat together with a coyote – landsakes – I mean,
this name, Daniel De Leon. De Leon for years already has his Thanks-
giving turkey plucked pulled and trussed: you think he'll let the rest of
you come into his kitchen and help him fire his stove? No sir.

Haywood Maybe no maybe yes. We got no choice but give him the choice.

We're either capitalists or revolutionists: and them capitalists are banded together like wolves in a bad winter. If wolves can do it, men can do it, and we're men, we ain't no sheep. So we put a bait out for De Leon and anyone of his views: we invite him to this conference to discuss ways and means of uniting the working people *on correct revolutionary principles*. For me there ain't no such word as *correct*: the only adjective I know about revolution is *successful* – but De Leon is De Leon and we got no choice but bring him in. Will you do that, Gene, get the invites out?

Debs I see it, I see it grow, the birth of freedom, the dawn of brotherhood, the beginning of mankind!

Haywood Sssh-ssh-ssh – we're overheard . . .

Exeunt.

SCENE 8

Enter DE LEON *and* SLP PARTY OFFICIALS, *and take their places for the convention.*

The hall fills. CONNOLLY *enters to take his modest seat.*

Connolly The convention is in session.
The inevitable procession
Of resolutions, amendments, determinations to retrench
Passes over my unheeding head as I sit here upon this bench:

I'm very well aware they're coming along to me personally – item twenty-seven on this morning's agenda, 'Consideration of the conduct of Comrade J. Connolly, Troy branch, etcetera etcetera . . .' Enough by itself to put a man's concentration into a state of random flux: but there's another thing – my wife Lillie – she was supposed to be arriving at Ellis Island last week on the Cunard boat from Liverpool and I met the boat and she wasn't on it – sure the last I heard from Dublin was she'd been ill but was now better – I mean very ill – could she have had a relapse? Neither letter nor telegram . . . what's he talking about now . . . ?

De Leon (*who has been conducting the convention all this while*) We come to item twenty-seven.

Connolly and De Leon (*together*) Consideration of the conduct of Comrade J. Connolly, Troy branch, etcetera etcetera . . .

De Leon In view of the gravity of the political tasks before us . . .

De Leon and Connolly (*together*) It is not proposed to waste much time upon this trivial matter . . .

De Leon But –

Connolly and De Leon (*together*) More confusion than it's worth among the rank and file of the party has been caused by the controversy . . .

De Leon Let me briefly sum it up. Comrade Connolly in his letter to *The*

Weekly People April ninth, nineteen hundred and four, wrote as follows, 'The theory that a rise in prices – '

De Leon and Connolly (*together*) 'Always destroys the value of a rise in wages sounds very revolutionary, but it is not true . . .'

De Leon (*as if this is all part of the quote*) Of course, if it's not true, then the foundations of the party doctrine rest on a basic falsehood, and if the foundations of the – –

Connolly (*interrupts*) Comrade De Leon, I did not write *that*! I demand you make clear what you are quoting from my letter and what you add on yourself as a gloss!

Chairman (*seated next to* DE LEON) The interruption is out of order.

Connolly So the interruption and every other interruption I could offer was out of order. So he tore me shreds. So I think myself damn lucky to be let off at that. He sums up. Oh, I'm off: what the hell has happened to Lillie. . . . ?

De Leon We will proceed with item twenty-eight: the request from Comrade Haywood of the Western Federation of Miners that the Socialist Labor Party demonstrate in practical form the solidarity we have already expressed for his union's courageous struggle. I would emphasise at this point that the doors of this convention are now closed and that the subsequent business under discussion is highly confidential and not to be revealed to anyone outside the party.

Sensation. CONNOLLY, *about to leave, resumes his seat, amazed.*

Comrade Haywood's overt request contains an inner meaning known only heretofore to the members of your National Executive Committee. I will now disclose it. At a meeting held in Chicago at which I was present, at which Comrade Haywood was present, and at which Comrade Debs of the Socialist Party was also present – –

Sensation.

a manifesto was drawn up announcing the formation of a totally new labour organisation, provisionally entitled 'The Industrial Workers of the World'.

Renewed sensation.

Yes. Wait a moment. 'The working class and the employing class have nothing in common . . . between these two classes a struggle must go on until all the toilers come together on the political as well as on the industrial field and take and hold that which they produce by their labor through an economic organisation of the working class, without affiliation with any political party.' I am quoting from the provisional terms of the manifesto. You will wonder perhaps how I could have put my name to a document that denies the possibility of affiliation to any political party? Don't it leave the SLP, my friends, just a little bit in the cold? My friends, don't it leave the Socialist Party of America much more permanently frozen hard in the arctic blizzards of their own impotence? Moreover, this new body will not confine itself to existing unions. We intend to create out of it an entire syndicate of the dispossessed: to include beneath the panoply of its united national strength all those millions and millions of unorganised migrant labourers who at present are protected by no organisation, and who likewise are affected by no political doctrine, save the deeply-felt bitterness of their miserable exploitation! In the Industrial Workers of the World, the one party involved that possesses a precise doctrine will be the one and only party in the end to achieve the allegiance of this hitherto amorphous mass.

A Member Say, comrade, d'you mean you think there's a chance we can take over the whole damn thing!

DE LEON *smiles and stands silent.*

Ovation. Exeunt all save CONNOLLY.

GOMPERS *crosses over, as though eavesdropping.*

Gompers (*to audience*)
Secret session, closed doors, windows locked and barred –
Communication in the direction of Big Bill Haywood, the word
is heard . . . ?
Haywood, Debs, De Leon, three men in a leaking tub:
So what gives, these two wiseguy socialists get their scrawny
backs a stiff rub
From a Colorado maverick with four bull's hoofs and a blinded
eye?
Aint no kinda threat, no sweat –
Such a miserable mean medicine-show alive on its legs yet?
Ten years them Western miners had to lie themselves down and
die . . .
Take it easy, Sam, relax, *rigor mortis* gets well set
At its own speed and its own speed alone –
Law of nature, no two men have the same damn marrow in their
every bone.
Exit.

SCENE 9

Connolly 'The Industrial Workers of the World' . . . ! 'The working class and the employing class have nothing in common' . . . nothing! Every ship that comes in brings more and more to fill our ranks: I can smell it, I can feel it – oh let my family be amongst them . . .

Enter IMMIGRATION OFFICIALS *and* PASSENGERS *arriving.*

1st Official Cunard passengers from Liverpool, this way now, let's have some order. D'ye hear me at the back there, if you don't speak no English don't try and speak at all, then we ain't in no danger of no misunderstanding – get that? No spikka da English, no spikka da nutt'n – okay? Fathers with families this side of the barrier, single men in the middle, women and kids on their own to the left. . . .

As the IMMIGRANTS *are processed,* LILLIE *(supposed to be with children) comes along the line.*

Lillie Connolly – Mrs James Connolly . . .
2nd Official Where from?
Lillie Dublin.
2nd Official Dublin Ireland? Okay. Anyone here for Connolly – Connolly from Dublin Ireland?
Connolly Connolly – yes – here – !
3rd Official (*keeps them apart*) Oh it's you, is it? Ain't I seen you here before?
Connolly I've been here every day this week –
3rd Official Yeah sure, I remember you – you said a wife and six kids – she got six kids, this man's wife?
2nd Official (*calls over the heads of the crowd*) Ain't your lucky day, mac, there's a woman here with five kids, but – –
Connolly No – wait a minute, let me past – *please*! Lillie! Lillie!
2nd Official Wait a moment, lady, I don't have your destination.
Lillie *Please!* I'm going to Troy –
2nd Official Troy Alabama, Troy Idaho, Troy Iowa, Troy Kansas, Troy Montana, Troy New York, Troy Ohio, Troy Pennsylvania, or Troy Vermont?
Lillie Troy New York – oh please, there's my husband –
2nd Official Then why can't you say so, d'ya wanna keep me here till Washington's Birthday? Okay, pass along – Next!
Connolly (*bursts past* OFFICIAL *and getting to her at last*) Lillie – ! Why, what's happened? Where's – where's Mona?
Lillie Oh, James, Mona's gone . . . The day before we were due to leave Dublin I sent her to her auntie's house to pick up some messages. She was left alone in the kitchen there. She thought she would surprise her auntie by making the tea for her. She put the kettle on, when it began to boil she tried to lift it. The handle was hot. She took a corner of her pinafore, to hold it with, you see: the other corner flew into the fire and caught alight. Every bit of her was burnt, every bit except her face, even inside of her, James, she was all burnt, she took twenty-four hours to die . . . you see, with the corner of her pinafore, she tried to hold the hot handle. That's why we couldn't come last week on the boat we said we'd come . . .

Exeunt PASSENGERS *and* OFFICIALS.

SCENE 10

Enter HAYWOOD, *to be suddenly hemmed in by* LABOUR DETECTIVES. *They have their guns out, he makes to draw his own pistol, but one of them is behind him and holds a gun in his back.*

1st Detective Haywood – !

2nd Detective Billy Boy, we got the drop on you, don't move, son, or you're blasted.

1st Detective You wanna know what it's about, Billy? You ever heard of a man called Steunenberg?

2nd Detective He was Governor of Idaho, he was in cahoots with all the mine-owners, he was an enemy of the union, and he's dead and you killed him.

1st Detective Killed him dead, Billy Boy, with a bomb: or if not you, personal; then Butch Cassidy and the Wild Bunch, they're on your payroll and you paid 'em: and for that you're gonna *fry*! Take him.

Haywood It's a frame-up!

They take him out.

NEWSBOYS *run in calling out headlines.*

Newsboys Fiendish conspiracy! Fiendish Conspiracy! – Big Bill Haywood charged with murder – Charles Moyer and George Pettibone accused with Haywood – Miners' Union linked with revolutionary bandits – death plot charges stun national labour leaders – 'It's a Frame-up' yells Haywood – Idaho lawmen reveal confession of co-conspirators – Haywood, Moyer and Pettibone for electric chair, D A urges . . . *etcetera etcetera. . . .*

Connolly (*hastily snatches a newspaper*) Frame-up, it must be a frame-up – of *course* it's a frame-up! The Pinkerton Detectives ran an *agent provocateur* into the union and had Steunenberg murdered themselves.

Enter SLP MEMBERS, *in excitement, and severally. All shouting:* '*Haywood is framed!*' '*Agent provocateur*', '*They're trying to break the union!*', *etcetera . . .*

1st Member (*to* CONNOLLY) There's an extraordinary general meeting of the New York State branches, comrade, tonight – Comrade De Leon in the chair – pass the word –

Connolly (*and others, pass the word*) Socialist Labor Party emergency meeting tonight – Comrade De Leon in the chair – all members without fail to attend if they can – Godsake, it's up to us to move three times as fast as they do!

A banner reading 'Free the Idaho Three' is brought in at the back. Amidst cheering and slogan-shouting DE LEON *takes his place in front of it. The meeting is all ready for him.*

De Leon Never in my entire life as a socialist organiser have I been confronted with such overt intimidation, with a provocation so bare-faced! 'Moyer and Haywood suspected of fiendish conspiracy'? There has indeed been a fiendish conspiracy: its aim has been two-fold – to break the miners' strike and to stultify at birth the Industrial Workers of the World! In token of which this evening I have invited on to the platform of the Socialist Labor Party none other than a man whom the capitalist enemies of our class fondly hoped would remain for ever excluded from these premises: comrades – Eugene Debs: of the Socialist Party of America!

Enter DEBS, *to vast applause.*

Comrade Debs and I have had our differences. In this emergency I prefer to sum them up thus – what he can do, I can't, and what I can do, he can't ... Comrade Debs, the floor is yours.

Debs Can do or can't – in this emergency, brothers, there's no question – the only thing we have to consider as what we *must* do: and must do it *now*! Okay, so the Idaho lawmen attempt to terrify the people with the threat of revolution – there may well be a revolution – I know that I for one will do all in my power to precipitate it!

Connolly (*jumps up in the midst of all the applause*) By direct action, Comrade Debs, and by *organisation*! I suggest at once that defence committees be formed from as wide a spectrum of workers' groups as is immediately practicable. Our own arrangements for printing and distribution of propaganda should be thrown open without restriction to the general effort – –

De Leon Yes. . . .

Everyone is excited after CONNOLLY's *outburst, though* DE LEON *is seen to be a little sceptical and calculating.*

Why not indeed? This party already, I am glad to say, has the machinery ready for precisely such a situation. Comrade Connolly, for example, I am quite certain would be capable of taking charge of all activities to secure the release of the Idaho Three in the area where he works . . . Troy, Comrade Connolly?

Connolly In point of fact I shall no longer be living in Troy. Newark, New Jersey.

De Leon Then let me recommend to the party branch in Newark New Jersey that Comrade Connolly be appointed forthwith to this onerous task.

He comes down and shakes CONNOLLY *by the hand.*

My friend, you'll have a great deal of work to do, and so little time for unproductive speculation . . . And that too applies to all of us – we have a revolutionary objective – if we fail to achieve it, the only possible alternative is the destruction of all socialism throughout the United States.

Debs On my way to this hall today I stopped off to visit the railroad men at the New York Central roundhouse. The news from Idaho had already reached them – I'm an old railroad man myself and, next to telegraph operators, we get hold of everything first – and already they had begun to sing. No, it wasn't exactly Puccini – but it meant what it said and it said what it meant.

He sings:

> If Moyer and Haywood die
> If Moyer and Haywood die
> Twenty million working-men
> Will know the reason why – !

General singing and the hall is emptied amidst immense excitement. CONNOLLY *gathers* LILLIE *to his arms and supports her: they go out after the crowd.*

END OF ACT 1

ACT 2: Out of the Party

SCENE 1

Immigrants arriving in the USA from a ship; with the Statue of Liberty, watchful police, and skyscrapers filling the background, so that little or no sky is visible. (Backcloth 6.)

The wide open spaces of America, mountain, desert and farmland, with groups of workers with red flags confronting armed posses of sheriffs' deputies, Ku Klux Klan etc. (Backcloth 7.)

Enter GOMPERS.

Song 'If Moyer and Haywood die' etc chanted by crowd off.

Gompers (*sings*)
>If Moyer and Haywood die
>If Moyer and Haywood die
>Twenty million working men
>Will know the reason why . . .

Moyer and Haywood, Moyer, Haywood, and Pettibone – born losers all three of 'em, born to squat on the hotseat for a trumped-up charge of murder in the boondocks of Idaho: which is where they're at right now and where to God I wish they'd stay! Yet hysteria we are now given, demagogic diarrhoea yet, to run around ourselves like hosepipes, tear the Idaho Pentitentiary brick-by-brick apart in the name of liberty . . . every loudmouth in the nation now restricts *my* liberty with the call for it! Only one purpose to be served by either hearing it or playing deaf: the quickest way to break the Industrial Workers of the World and the Miners' Federation and at the same time preserve the AF of L with its reputation unsmirched for the safeguarding of human rights . . . ?

While he has been talking, two of his AFL OFFICIALS *have come in and adopted obsequious postures.*

1st Official Haywood and Moyer and the third guy this Pettibone, the three of 'em is working men, and working men should be supported by an organisation of working men. Boss, I speak only as my two ears have heard, from our membership is all.

2nd Official Such membership, boss, is solid respectable American family men, pay their taxes, pay their mortgages, Sundays they go to church – hell they don't wanna be mixed up defending no dynamite-bombers alleged have slain a state governor!

Gompers *Ex*-state governor: in cahoots with the mine-owners: he *deserved* it: did they *do* it? Sure we all know the slogan of the IWW is 'the working class and the employing class have nuth'n in common' – but assassination . . . ? Could be . . .

1st Official On the other hand, boss, could be, it is, as claimed, a frame-up . . .

Gompers Big Bill Haywood is an *anarchist* – he's a *socialist* – he's a *red* – he is everything I *hate*! Do I have to stick my neck out and tell the world that such a bum should be totally innocent of what I know in my heart he would dearly love to do to *me*?

2nd Official So we hold off from the defence campaign, and we don't say nuth'n – sealed lips?

Gompers You gotta better policy? So serve up a better policy. Meantime Sam Gompers keeps his trap shut, but tight.

Enter ELIZABETH GURLEY FLYNN.

1st Official You got an appointment? Mr Gompers don't see nobody without an appointment.

Flynn Mr Gompers will see me: I'm from the IWW. I came here to speak to you about the Idaho trial.

Gompers It figgers . . .

Flynn Mr Gompers, we need you: the American working class in their hour of national crisis need – –

GOMPERS *snaps his fingers at his* OFFICIALS *who retire.*

Gompers Little lady . . . sealed lips. Who am I to try to prejudice the course of justice with reckless comment?

Flynn You think no reckless comment has already been made? Why, the president himself –

Gompers Has delivered an opinion in his wiser moments he will regret. We all know that Mr Roosevelt is the lackey hireling of the Wall Street barons – now and then I read the newspapers, even *your* newspapers, that surprise you? But in this office, *I'm* the president: non-political, unaffiliated, the interests of the hard-working American wage-earner is all. Which in my book is not compatible with the agitation of subversive reds. On the other hand, I stand for justice . . .

Flynn *I* stand for justice and I'm a red, I'm not ashamed of it.

Gompers That at your age you should be so certain . . . ? Say, kid, do you know what in these circles is the name we give the Industrial Workers of the World? We call 'em Wobblies – if you like, Inexperienced Wobblies of the Wild – because you wobble: between the gun and the camp-meeting, between Dodge City and Moscow Russia, between wanting to build Jerusalem and not knowing how to stop yourselves falling down with the walls of Jericho: hell, you're young and you're new and you're not ashamed of nuth'n. Now look here, child, I'm old: and I guess I *am* ashamed of it. I guess poor old Sam Gompers hates like hell to see three good men walk head-high into Death Row, and just for a mess of politics, there ain't nuth'n he can do for 'em, nuth'n . . . Kid, am I on the way out – am I a has-been? Does Big Bill Haywood send me children, like my own daughters, to prove to me my course is run? . . . now wait a minute, there's no-one here, I sent Jake down to the printing-shop to see about some committee rosters, oh child, I'm telling you, you've twisted and twined Sam Gompers up and down your wide white thigh, for God's sake let him put his eyes on where his heart has already reached, put his eyes, put his poor old fingers – –

Flynn I'll break your poor old fingers off like a pair of used matchsticks.

Gompers You would? . . . She would . . . Goddammit, child, you don't believe I'd try a dirty thing like that? Okay, Wobbly, on your way. You done your good deed for the day.

She is about to go out, scornfully, but 2ND OFFICIAL *has entered and silently blocks her way.*

And now I'm gonna do mine. For Haywood and his associates, justice: nuth'n but justice! The AFL will call for it! Sam Gompers' word is gold, girl: no need to answer me – on your way.

She goes out, dumbfounded.

2nd Official Boss, do you mean to tell me . . . ?

Gompers My friend, I had my hand around her pretty little butt and she wouldn't let it stay there! Brought the tears into my eyes.

2nd Official And for that you . . . ?

A phone is heard ringing, off . . .

Gompers For that I took good care, Al, to let it stand hard in her fiery mind that the AF of L comes into this campaign nervous, undecided, without initiative, quite happy to let the Wobblies and the socialists make the running! That we got no kind of strategy – for the blood-beat of a prudish broad I personally would sell out all the deals I ever made with both Wall Street and the government! And with that she's gonna bring her friends into competition with us, in public? With all that they're three parts beaten before they've even entered the ring.

Enter 1ST OFFICIAL.

1st Official Hey, boss, on the telephone – Washington – it's the White House, no less!

Gompers I'll take it in here. For Teddy Roosevelt I should wear a tuxedo? In my shirt-sleeves! Gimme the phone.

He talks into telephone.

Gompers here, AF of L . . . Mr President! . . . Yeah . . . Yeah . . . Okay, Mr President, I read the message, sir, I read it good – how far is the present frenzy among labour organisations a genuine response to injustice in Idaho: or is it but a prelude to the same state of chaos like is happening in Russia? . . . Mr President, I read the newspapers, and I know very well that what's happening in Russia nineteen-hundred-zero-five is an overt and planned attempt to overthrow the Czarist tyranny. And for why do they overthrow it? Because a genuine response to injustice in Petrograd was met by the bloodstained Cossacks with a volley of shot, that's why! . . . Mr President, you have spoken – I read it in my newspaper, an exceedingly rash statement, sir, that prematurely assumed Haywood's guilt: and I am, as of right now, holding back my unions from a catastrophic public outburst that would make Petrograd look like popcorn! If I have to join with the IWW in alleging the Idaho trial to be an unprincipled frame-up, then American democracy will have found itself a *soviet* from which to publicise its grievances! Mr President, such bad news, sir, and for me just as much as for you. . . . Mr President, who said anything about 'convinced of their innocence'? A fair trial, with honest testimony, prove them guilty or not guilty according to the constitution. If the verdict goes against them, let the socialists carry the odium of having proclaimed it a frame-up: but if it turns out they *are* innocent, then government and responsible labour take credit together for preparing the simple justice that delivered them from their ordeal. Sure there's wide spectacular speeches Sam Gompers will spout out in this forthcoming campaign: but not one demand in them larger than what his own president has guaranteed . . . So we both know where we stand. I thank you, Mr President! I am so grateful you see it my way – and I'm honoured, sir, most honoured . . .

He rings off.

Now then: in the meantime. With their leaders in jail, the Western Federation of Miners is chopped off at the neck: and the cadaver is open for bids: so we bid. I want our people in charge of that self-styled wildcat union by the end of next month. If there's gotta be an election, then fix the election. If shotguns and hoodlums is in order, then indent for them as per the usual contractors – but just you make damn sure you don't let me hear you do it. The minute we get control we yank them mule-faced miners clear outta the IWW, horse, harness, axle and lynch-pins, and pull 'em back into the AF of L. Get it?

1st Official Got it.

Gompers So go to Colorado – don't stop by at no whore-houses – I want work, boy, I want it smart!

Exit 1ST OFFICIAL.

Al, you go to Idaho. Get an entree into the jail: and see what you can make of softening up Moyer. You gotta make him believe that if his buddy Bill Haywood hadn't a been so damnfool reckless in linking with all them socialists, then nobody woulda railroaded the poor sap the way they have.

2nd Official Guess that ain't no fairy-tale, boss: it's plain true.

Gompers Okay, so get with Moyer and tell him the plain truth. If he comes innocent out of court, I want him *my* man: no more a Wobbly! Get it?

2nd Official Got it.

Gompers Go.

Exit 2ND OFFICIAL.

Sings:

> My name is Samuel Gompers and the direction of my movement
> Is never where you think it goes but always at a tangent:
> Up the town the sun shines bright and down the town its
> raining –
> Galoshes in my pocket-flap, I will not be complaining . . .

Exit with a little dance.

SCENE 2

A scene in the dark. Campfire. HOBOES. *Train noises in the distance.*

Hoboes (*sing*)
> When springtime has come
> O won't we have fun
> We'll git out of jail
> And we'll go on the bum –
> Hallelujah I'm a bum
> Hallelujah, bum again
> Hallelujah, give us a handout
> To revive us again . . .

Enter IWW ORGANISER.

IWW Organiser Howdy, friends – I'm half-frozen, travelled over the Sierra twelve hours through a blizzard, riding an open coal train from Sacramento – you got coffee? Trade you a can of beans for it.

1st Hobo Put your beans in the stewpan, pardner, take your whack of what's made of it.

IWW Organiser I got holes in my coat and patches in my pants but the only thing that keeps me warm is a little pink card in the heel of my sock . . . Am I talking to my friends?

2nd Hobo Boys, pull your cards out, show them to the man. Okay, mister, ride it easy, we're all IWW here. What's the news from Sacramento?

IWW Organiser From Sacramento the news is great. Money for the defence of Haywood and Moyer taken in by the bucketful. You look at the back of my card, you see I'm entitled to collect. You won't have a dollar, so gimme a quarter, you won't have a quarter, so gimme a dime –

Sings:

> If Moyer and Haywood die
> If Moyer and Haywood die
> There's twenty million working men
> Will know the reason why . . .

Rattle of money contributed.

IWW Organisers (*at all corners of the stage*) You won't have a dollar so gimme a quarter, you won't have a quarter, so gimme a dime. . . .

Song repeated and taken up all round in the dark and rattle of money.

Debs (*in the dark*) This Idaho trial is the greatest legal battle in American history. Already from trade unionists and members of socialist parties more than sixty thousand dollars have been collected to fight for the cause.

The songs and collections continue . . .

1st Reporter (*in the dark*) Protest parades held in every major city of the entire United States. In San Francisco the corrupt motives of the prosecution were laid bare by a phalanx of platform orators, addressing the largest crowd ever seen in the streets of the city.

2nd Reporter (*in the dark*) Fifty thousand men marched chanting through the streets of Boston Massachusetts.

1st Reporter Twenty thousand persons in double file paraded uptown from the Lower East Side of New York City. At Fortieth and Lexington they merged and continued to Grand Central Palace where John Chase, Morris Hillquit and Joshua Wanhope proclaimed Haywood's innocence and reiterated 'Frame-up!'

General Cries Frame-up: frame-up: frame-up!

Debs President Roosevelt has alleged that Bill Haywood before trial is already a guilty man! We protested in the strongest terms the illegality of the president's statement: he has now taken space in the newspapers to deny he ever said it! I say he thus stands pilloried before the American people! If he continues to attempt to deny it, I shall convict him with the proof! Nevertheless, his denial, hypocritical though it may be, is the first decisive victory for organised labour in the kidnapping battle of the class war in the United States –

Tremendous cheers. Continued singing.

De Leon (*in the dark*) Comrade Debs and the Socialist Party, myself and the Socialist Labor Party, William Haywood in his jail cell and the Western Federation of Miners he created are together against all odds, and against all odds we shall march forward! Comrades, give your money, without stint, for this noble struggle!

Cheers, more calls for money, more collecting, more singing.

Urgent Cries Watch it boys, it's the Pinkerton men – it's the Pinkerton men and the Feds – get the hell outa here, scram, boys, the Feds is coming!

Police Voice (*with bullhorn*) I am declaring this meeting a prohibited assembly: if the area is not cleared my peace officers have orders to break up the crowd by force!

Confusion; excitement; anger; scuffling. Then a violent charge by the peace officers. Screams, casualties, and the stage is cleared. Lights come up.

SCENE 3

Enter CONNOLLY.

Connolly Transported, exalted, to Newark New Jersey,
    On the hard wind of these new politics comes the Irishman
      Connolly –

I'm on the Press and Literature Committee of the New Jersey Socialist Labor Party: I'm controlling and co-ordinating the Newark Working-men's Defense Committee: with our sometime bitter rivals of the American Socialist Party I am on a full dozen committees and sub-committees for the propagation and extension of the Industrial Workers of the World – I've got a contact-group set up to explore relations with the Newark locals of the AFL! I've even got the use of the AF of L union-halls to hold meetings, distribute literature, and present petitions for the release of the Idaho Three.

LILLIE *has entered as he speaks, and stands at the other side, speaking directly to the Audience without reference to Connolly.*

Lillie No work for him in Troy after the strike in the shirt-industry: his removal to Newark a most perilous speculation on the strength only that he thought there were one or two in this town whom he knew who could put the word out for him: all the weeks we have been here, nothing. He has his politics, and in the meanwhile he trudges as always round the 'situations vacant'. It's no part of my game to sit in the kitchen and wait for him. Sure I did that enough and to spare in the old days in Dublin: we are here, in the New World, and the word they all tell me is 'hustle'. So I did: and I did discover – for a woman with a needle and enough time on her hands there is everything from ball gowns to dust-covers to be taken in on a piecework contract and hemmed and stitched till my hot eyeballs dissolve down the fold of my cheek. I say nothing about the pay that's offered – measured in cents – but by the week's end it can sometimes add up into dollars. You don't believe I tell him about it – he sees the children at school and their food on the table, and that's enough for him in his present state, as he organises the starving millions. But if he doesn't get work soon at least one of the children will be forced to go out and get hold of it in his place. And if that happens he will never stand for it: I'll have no choice but to deceive him. Not hard: look at him now. He hasn't even noticed I'm here, let alone what I'm doing...

During the above speeches, CONNOLLY *has been engaged in a constant bustle of party activists and union organisers – messages, money, piles of pamphlets and newspapers etc.* LILLIE *has been similarly engaged receiving bundles of garments and lingerie, which she is arranging in piles and laying out her spools of thread etc. When she has done this to her satisfaction, she goes out with all her work.*

Connolly Will you look at me – I'm flat broke:
    No money in my pocket and where the hell can I get work?
    Try my luck as I did, before, with the insurance companies: no
      luck.
    Carried tiles up a ladder for a craftsman on a roof: no luck: I
      fell off.
    No union card, except the pink one in the heel of my left sock –
    And that one will feed no family: more like it will break my
      back...

A Party Worker (*Irish, comes up to him*) Jim, at the news-stand at the corner of Eighteenth Street – the feller there won't take our papers because he says that there's no demand. It's a lie.

Connolly It's a lie, sure, he's in fear of the police: don't I know the man, a sound commercial argument would convert him in two minutes. He wants a demand, so create a demand. Send six or eight of our friends to ask for the paper one after another on their way home from work this evening – and the moment the last one in the line has put the question you follow it up once more with the offer of your bundle. Won't he jump at it?

Party Worker In the nature of a bluff?

Connolly It's worked before: it'll work again...

PARTY WORKER *goes off, laughing, singing, 'Yes sir, that's my baby ...'*

Sure the whole of American capitalism uses no other technique...

Sings:

    Yes sir that's my baby
    Yes sir, that's the way we
    Roll the dollars
    Roll the dollars
    Roll the dollars, roll....

Sure the whole of American capitalism claims itself to be nothing but the promotion of the individial – we say enterprise – we say bluff – so why the devil not? Public library first of all. Take a look at the daily papers...

From a newspaper rack he selects a paper and pores over the columns.

'Wanted, skilled machinists for Singer Sewing-Machine plant.' So we go forward to the bookshelves . . .

Library Assistant What's your pleasure, sir, can I help you?

Connolly I fancy, ma'am, I'd get enormous pleasure from a technical discourse upon sewing-machine manufacture. You wouldn't, I suppose, have – –

Library Assistant Indeed we have, sir, here it is. In connection with the Singer Company I guess? That sure is an invention put New Jersey on the map!

Connolly (*with book*) So let's hope that James Connolly finds his geographical position as decisively determined . . . Yes . . . Yes . . . It's not impossible . . . We say enterprise . . . We say bluff . . .

He wanders about, reading over to himself little splurges of technical jargon, and memorising things on his fingers' ends.

Yet I know from the start it'll never come off
If they take me for a tile-hanger who got scared at one steep roof!

He thinks for a moment, then starts rapidly to change his appearance.

Gotta go there like I look like I know everything that I do not know:
Razzmatazz, go get it, boy, go get up and go!

He puts himself into a loud checked jacket, clip-on bow-tie, flat straw hat etc., and caps the effect with a cigar.

I never smoked in my life. Should I chew it? What the hell . . .

He retires as Singer's MANAGER *and* SECRETARY *enter.*

Manager You're late, doll, don't apologise, an apology's a sign of weakness, got your pad, got your pencil, take a letter.
'For attention Mr Blumenkrantz, Chickabiddy Camisole Company, Seventh Avenue, New York. Hi!'

Secretary Hi?

Manager Sure – hi – why not? Ikey Blumenkrantz is an old buddy of mine, do you want I should alienate the guy before I break him in two? So write it down –
'Hi! Ikey I am sore at you. But plenty. Complaints through your lawyer against alleged treddle-defects in the seven Singer machines model forty-three dispatched to your plant as per enclosed schedule are herewith repudiated. Now listen, Ikey, get this good – '

CONNOLLY *sets his hat at a sharp angle; puffs, with nausea, on his cigar; squares his shoulders; and strides forward.*

Connolly Mr Schmidtkopf? Please don't rise! I won't take thirty seconds of your valuable time. Now, sir, I understand you have a vacancy in this plant for a qualified machinist – ?

Manager Say, have you an appointment?

Connolly Sir, a man with an appointment is a man with time to waste: and I well know that Singer Sewing Machines got no time for wasters! They tell me, sir, your clients have trouble with the treddle-connections of your model forty-three?

Manager They tell you – who tells you? Why, goddammit, that's a trade secret!

Connolly (*aside to audience*) If you want to keep secrets, don't dictate in a high-pitched bellow. Lesson Number One for political subversives . . . (*To* MANAGER) Now this here, sir, I take it, is your model forty-three? *He approaches a sewing-machine mounted for display. Aside to audience:* If it isn't, I'm done. But thank goodness it has a number plate on it. Lesson Number Two: under conditions of expanding industrial economy, the capitalist adversary has as yet felt no need to conceal his intentions. Read, mark, learn, and *don't* do likewise. Bear in mind what happened to Haywood – tough and rough but a foredoomed loudmouth.

He has turned the machine over and is activating the moving parts.

(*To* MANAGER) Yes indeed, Mr Schmidtkopf, there's a definite indication that the left-hand treddle-bearing is inclined to run sticky. Have you checked the possibility that the bore-gauge of this casting is a millimetre too narrow?

(*Aside to audience*) Lesson Number Three: never forget your adversary is quite as much a blind eedjit as you yourself would have been in the same situation. He hadn't checked the bore-gauge.

(*To* SECRETARY) Now if you, my dear, will hold the female component of the double-activating screw-manifold, I'll take the other end and ease it through, so, till we've worked it clear of the bed-trunnion. Bully for you. Can I trouble you, Mr Schmidtkopf, to get a good grip on the treddle itself so it don't slide out of its housing, I apply a small file to the metalwork at the joint. . . . Bully. One millimetre. No more. . . . There we are, that should do it. Right y'are, then how does she ride? . . . Oh bully bully hot dog, Mr Schmidtkopf! You can write Mr Blumenkrantz this minute, sir, tell him call his lawyers off, tell him cash on delivery rush his male components express back here to Newark, you shave off them one millimetre circumference with your power-lathe, return them to New York the same day carriage-paid: and Mr Schmidtkopf, you both are saved one helluva lotta grief!

Manager Why, say, boy, that's not bad! Why, hell, not bad at all! Angelina, re-write that letter just like the man said. Say, I don't know what your name is, who the hell cares what your name is – you understand sewing-machines: that's all that concerns me!

Connolly Am I hired?

Manager Goddammit, man, of course you're hired!

Exeunt MANAGER *and* SECRETARY.

Connolly Lesson Number Four: sharp practice by itself will avail you nothing unless it's backed by a solid foundation of theory . . . Likewise without practice, the best theory in the world droops and dies before it's blossomed. No danger of that these days with the Socialist Labor Party – no sir, in Newark no longer dare they call us an impracticable talking-shop – upon the streets, among the people, like an avalanche – we have *moved*!

SCENE 4

The stage fills with people, all greeting each other in different languages – Italian, German, Russian, etc. A lot of red flags and one large banner saying 'Freedom for the Idaho Three' and 'Freedom of Speech in Newark'. The 'Internationale' is sung, in several different languages. ELIZABETH GURLEY FLYNN *and the Irish* PARTY WORKER *join* CONNOLLY.

Party Worker There's already twenty thousand Italians in Cutler Street.

Flynn I've got the Irish crowd contained three blocks back down Seventh Avenue. I should think at least eight thousand.

Connolly I'd have hoped there'd be more Germans. What's happened to the Germans?

Party Worker Don't you know their committee insisted they should march in step to a brass band? I think they're still forming fours on the recreation field with a serjeant-major, but don't worry – they've all turned out!

Connolly I'll bet the Italian Socialist Federation never thought when they began this protest that every bloody nationality in Newark would be joining them in such numbers – Lizzie, begod, it's a roman triumph we have here and no error!

Flynn And none but yourself is responsible for it, Mr Connolly.

Party Worker Wouldn't you call it a class of a disgrace, though, the Italians had to begin it? How come that they have got their own socialist group and we the Irish are left nowhere?

Connolly You might well say how come. What's done once can be done once more: and we'll do it!

He indicates a PINKERTON MAN, *to one side of the stage.*

Pinkerton Man (*scribbles in notebook*) 'To the Pinkerton Detective Agency – Operator's Report Number Q seventy-six. So far no violence. Good-humoured assembly of unprecedented crowds none the less contains trouble-making potential assessed at grade sixteen on regular agency scale. No weapons overtly carried. Flags: red.' For some reason the word's just come down from head office: no repeat no provocation in Newark . . .

He crosses over to another vantage point, passing an AF OF L OFFICIAL *as he does so.*

AF of L Official Pinkerton man, huh? I wish to God this Haywood guy was acquitted or hanged or sump'n. All manner of Micks and Wops running in and out of my AF of L local every day with their damn leaflets – there's nuth'n I can do to stop 'em since the word came down from head office – accord all repeat all facilities to associated groups in Haywood campaign – d'you suppose that Sam Gompers has gone completely loco?

Intensified cheering and music.

Connolly It's the Germans, they've arrived! Okay, we start the speeches.

He mounts the rostrum. He speaks first in German, then Italian. He does not know these tongues well, but has been carefully coached and pleases the crowd immensely with his humorous acceptance of his own poor pronunciation.

Willkommen die Kameraden der Vereinigung der Sozialisten Deutschlands an dieser historischen Gedenkfeier! Die Sozial Demokratische Partei Deutschlands, der nachfolger von Marx und Engels, ist der wegweiser Stern heutiger Sozialismus Europas. Langemöge sie leben!
Amici, fratelli, salutiamo il vostro corraggio e solidarti e il indomito volunta contra il represso di liberte delle parole. Siete un essempio e isperatoro a ogni lavoratoro in Newark e esperiamo da oggi che ogni lavoratoro in Newark serrà egualmente un isperatori a tutta gli stati uniti!
Comrades, fellow-workers, citizens of Newark: the Italian Socialist Federation last month in commemoration of the Paris Commune of eighteen hundred and seventy-one carried the red flag through these streets. With brutality that flag was confiscated by the Newark police. An outrage and a violation of the civil rights of American citizens to express without hindrance their legitimate political views. We want that flag back. The commissioner of police has told us repeatedly we're not going to get it back. Very well: so we've made some more!

Great cheering and waving of red flags.

Last year, in Russia, not in one city, but throughout the entire heart of that rotten yet malignant Empire, the example of the people of the Paris Commune was followed yet again. I have the privilege of introducing to you today an active participant in those tremendous events – for her own safety, she has no name – we will call her Comrade B., from the

Petrograd Workers' Soviet – she was arrested, she was exiled, she escaped – and here she is!

A RUSSIAN REVOLUTIONARY *appears on the rostrum to great cheering.*

Russian Revolutionary Father Gapon, the good priest, who at that time no-one knew was also a police spy, said to the poor people: 'Come, I will lead you to the Czar – the Czar is your little father, he will hear your cry and give you bread and deliver you from your affliction.' So thousands of them marched to the gates of the Czar's palace. The soldiers stepped forward, they brought their rifles to their shoulders, and – as a loving father disciplines his thoughtless children – they shot those people down. So after that it was nothing but the general strike – every factory in Russia was made desolate, closed and empty; it was the mutiny – the whole Black Sea Fleet was set at derision by the fury of the sailors of the ironclad 'Potemkin' – even the dreaded Cossacks for a time were without power to intimidate, to trample down the aroused and vengeful people... Yet here I am: a refugee. Not for ever: indeed not. But when our work is to be done again, and I go back to take part in it, we must have thoroughly understood the reasons for what went wrong. First: we were too spontaneous. Second: the industrial workers received little or no support from the broad mass of the rural peasantry. Third: and most important: there was no fully-informed cohesive party of the revolution to seize and hold the political leadership. It is from now on to be our task to correct these grave mistakes. I recommend you, American workers, to take heed of our disappointment, to relate the lessons of our struggle to your particular situation. Above all, remember this: the failure of a revolution is the springboard of the next success! Long live the heroic martyrs of the year of nineteen hundred and five! Long live the determined workers of the United States of America! Long live the Soviet Socialist Revolution in Russia, in America, and throughout the entire world!

During the cheers at the end of this speech the RUSSIAN *nervously pours herself out a drink of water – straight into* CONNOLLY'*s hat.*

Connolly (*among laughter*) I hope it won't shrink. It's the only one I have! Miss Elizabeth Gurley Flynn, who needs no introduction in Newark.

Flynn (*on the rostrum*) Paris, Russia – and now Idaho – we're on the go, we can't be stopped! The bosses know that their days of unquestioned power are now numbered. The Industrial Workers of the World is an aurora borealis that hangs blood-red in the sky above them – and in their terror they try anything to make the decent family people who support their local police turn and run like squealing piglets into the warm protective sty of the 'democratic process'. I suppose there's no-one in this place requires to be told the difference between a hog and a human being – –

Mother Jones (*interrupts from the back*) No lookit, Lizzie, honey, you got no call to go running down good healthy hogs! 'Cos I raised hogs and I raised human children, and I tell you in some respects them hogs has got the edge on us!

Flynn Brothers and sisters the oldest and the toughest fighter in the whole American labour movement! – Mother Jones, from the Illinois coalfields, from the Western Federation of Miners, from the Industrial Workers of the World!

Mother Jones (*mounts rostrum amidst cheers*) Midwinter in the mountains when every pond and creek is frozen, and there's four-legged critters everywhere can get nary a drop to drink, what does your hog do then? He ain't no slouch at finding out just where that water's got to – and nothing, brothers and sisters, *nothing* will hold him back from quenching his thirst. He sets his four sharp hooves splayed-out on the shining ice, and he bends his big strong head, and he bashes with that old snout of his, bang bang bang till the ice is cracked and broken and shivered into a thousand fragments! And that's what we're aiming to do, and it's what we *can* do, and it's what we *will* do, brothers and sisters, right now, bang bang bang, till Haywood Moyer and Pettibone is busted out of the Penitentiary and Old Man Grabitall and all his dirty dollars is busted out of the seat of government in Idaho and Colorado and Nevada and Montana and Washington DC! Say, gimme a flag there – yeah, we got this revolution – so let's get it upon the road!

She starts singing; everyone joins in and exeunt.

> If the boss gets in the way we're gonna roll it over him
> We're gonna roll it over him, we're gonna roll it over him
> If the boss gets in the way we're gonna roll it over him
> We're gonna roll the Union on . . .
> > *etcetera etcetera . . .*

SCENE 5

Enter DE LEON *and an* SLP PARTY OFFICIAL, *looking through letters.*

1st Party Official Queries, comrade De Leon, queries, forever queries –

De Leon From every branch in the country it seems –

1st Party Official What is exactly our relation with the Socialist Party? What is exactly our correct attitude to the IWW? How far can we go in association with the AFL? Is there not a danger of too diverse a collaborationism? Is it proper for our members to speak on the same platform as –

De Leon I thought on such points I had made myself perfectly clear?

1st Party Official Of course you have, comrade – but –

De Leon You know how to answer all these, do you not? Hello, what's this one?

1st Party Official Newark New Jersey . . . Branch secretary passes on a recommendation that the Newark Italian Socialist Federation be affiliated with the Socialist Labor Party.

De Leon En bloc? Certainly not!

1st Party Official It would mean a considerable and very welcome increase in our membership –

De Leon I've no doubt. And that's why. That's exactly why, comrade. Do you not appreciate the credentials of Italian socialism? Three-quarters anarchist: and the remaining one-fourth mafioso. Newark. Dear me, Newark . . . Comrade, I will unreservedly hand over to you five cents if the name of James Connolly is not somewhere in that letter.

1st Party Official You win. The whole thing seems to be his idea. He says, on account the Italians showed such spirit in their Paris Commune festival –

De Leon Ha! The Irish faction-fighter smelling blood on the end of his old shillelagh, wouldn't you guess it? And of course, as we well know, the Irish predilection for secret societies is even worse than the Italian. Are you familiar with the history of an occult cabal called the Irish Republican Brotherhood? Its 'secret melodramatic conspiratorial methods' – I quote Karl Marx – which have ended universally and inevitably in failure? Its invariable penetration by the informer and the police-agent? Its consistent vulnerability to the influence of the Catholic Church? Its – I won't go on. The answer is definitely 'no'.

1st Party Official Comrade, I don't know how you're going to take this: but he says – he says if we are prepared to accept the Italians, then maybe in due course we will also accept his *Irish* Socialist Federation –

De Leon His *what*! Oh my God. He has in fact formed such a body? In Newark?

1st Party Official It has been formed. And not only in Newark. He mentions New York, Boston, Buffalo, Baltimore . . . I don't think we issued any precise directive against it?

De Leon We did not. And we're not going to. I like to believe I have a *flexible* approach. But heaven knows, this must be stopped. How to do it . . . ? I know . . . Where's Comrade Zimmerman?

1st Party Official Zimmerman!

Enter 2ND PARTY OFFICIAL, *out of breath.*

Comrade De Leon . . .

2nd Party Official (*to* DE LEON) Yes, comrade?

De Leon Zimmerman, I want a member from a district well away from the metropolitan area of activities, who belongs to a non-English-speaking minority which is not known to possess any ethnic socialist grouping of its own: and who is able to write legibly and coherently upon the danger of centrifugal racial tendencies within the movement. Give me a name.

2nd Party Official Comrade Stromqvist, Arizona. He's a Swede. I guess he fills

all the requirements. He is in New York this week. Do you want me to – –
De Leon Request him to drop in and have a word with me: yes. He is to prepare a short paper for inclusion in *The Weekly People*. We will see if it is replied to by any individual from Newark New Jersey: and if it is: we go in for the kill.

Exeunt.

SCENE 6

Enter GOMPERS, GRABITALL *and* BOSSES.

Grabitall (*sings*)
> All around this great nation in fury they call
> For red revolution to be our downfall –
Chorus Revolution revolution revolution – take heed
> Revolution feeds fat on the food of our greed!
1st Boss (*sings*)
> We try to do good and make wealth and make growth
> But red revolution will swallow them both!
Chorus Revolution revolution revolution – take heed
> Revolution feeds fat on the food of our greed!
2nd Boss (*sings*)
> We've all gotta gather we've all gotta cling
> Each one to each other to beat off this thing.
Chorus Revolution revolution revolution – take heed
> Revolution feeds fat on the food of our greed!
3rd Boss (*sings*)
> Sam Gompers, Sam Gompers – we thought you our friend:
> Will you let revolution get us all in the end?
Gompers (*sings*)
> Revolution revolution I ain't Jesus Christ
> To bring out no miracle to save you your life!
Grabitall Wait a minute, now, that sentiment is detrimental to the cordial atmosphere that should prevail in this pan-American industrial management-labour good neighbour-relationship gathering! Mr Gompers, withdraw, please, your impertinent remark!
Gompers I come today to Newark because somebody writes to me that Singer Sewing-Machines Incorporated is hosting the gathering: and I find the prosperous city of Newark New Jersey struck flat in its own streets like a crazy man with a cut-throat razor!
2nd Boss And what the hell else? Are you too dumb to realise just what happened here last weekend! The red flag flown openly the full length of Seventh Avenue, flown openly and unhindered – not one Newark peace-officer so much as pulled out his night-stick! Moreover, it says here –

He is reading from a newspaper: all the others except GOMPERS have newspapers open as well.

– that a communist anarchist from Russia was allowed to freely advocate open mutiny in the armed forces!

Gompers Can I just ask you one little non-incriminating totally innocent question? Is your Singer Sewing-Machine Company a unionised plant or not?

2nd Boss Goddammit, that's not germane – !

3rd Boss Don't evade it: we got no time to play games: you damn fool, this is an emergency!

1st Boss Just answer the man, goddammit. Just explain to him the ingredients of your own stupid stewpot.

2nd Boss Lookit here, over my dead body will Singer Sewing-Machines become unionised!

Gompers And so you wonder why the hell I choose to question your credentials. You make me sick to my gut.

1st Boss It ain't only Newark – these Wobbly demonstrations are held over the length and breadth of the continent!

Bosses (*read out from newspapers*) Chicago – Philadelphia – Seattle – Cleveland – Detroit – New York City –

Gompers You think I don't know it? And you think I don't know why?
(*To* 1ST BOSS) Mr Senator: when you were elected to the legislature of this great republic, did you or did you not swear to be a friend to labour: and did you or did you not receive the sincere endorsement of the AF of L in that election?

3rd Boss Don't evade it!

2nd Boss Just answer the man, goddammit!

1st Boss Yeah.

Gompers Without our endorsement, do you reckon you coulda won?

1st Boss No.

Gompers And since the day you obtained office, upon what particular issue have you swung your political weight in favour of labour and against the Wall Street trusts? . . . Don't answer. We know the answer. The answer is not one! Not one lousy stinking Congressional motion – ! Any wonder that the wild-wood radicals, the Wobblies, the egalitarianising fanatic socialists have made such appalling gains!

Grabitall Say, I been reading the newspaper: the Newark newspaper: *your* sheet, Mr Chairman of the Singer Sewing-Machine Incorporated. You said, over your dead body would subversive combinations get a foothold in this plant? You said it maybe with the intention of talking kinda *tough*? So how come I see here that a Singer employee was in the middle of that socialistic *kaffeeklatch* last weekend on Seventh Avenue?

2nd Boss What, that's a goddam lie – I never – no – say, gimme that news-

paper! My God! Where's my manager! Schmidtkopf! Hey, Schmidtkopf, goddammit: get your feet inside this office!

Enter Singer MANAGER.

Schmidtkopf – *WHO IS CONNOLLY?* James Connolly, Singer
machinist – will you look at it, man, page five, column three – will you
look at it and then tell me – WHO THE HELL HIRED THAT HOOD-
LUM HERE!

1st Boss Wait a minute, what's that noise?

3rd Boss Why, it's right outside your entrance, there's a man making a speech
to the morning shift as they come off duty!

1st Boss He has a banner –

3rd Boss Can anyone read it – ?

Gompers Socialist Labor Party – Industrial Workers of the World –

CONNOLLY *has appeared in a far corner of the theatre with his banner,
addressing the workers.*

Connolly There is no law in this country that forbids a working man to
organise himself with his fellows into a legitimate labour union –

Bosses Schmidtkopf – !

Manager That's *him*!

Bosses Him – *who*?

Manager James Connolly!

Bosses and Grabitall James Connolly . . . !

Grabitall Gentlemen, I think the moral of this is clear to all. By the beginning
of next year, nineteen hundred and seven, men, women and kids in this
country'll be glad to get *any* work, any work at all for any rate under any
conditions – *I* seen it coming, Brother Gompers, so should you. Slump,
my friend, will mean there's a few mouths around here won't talk so
goddam uppity. Get it?

Gompers Got it. And get this. The working class don't make no slump. And
when slump comes, the working class is gonna fight against it, hard.
Remember – *my* membership could be *that* man's membership tomorrow
lunchtime – and if it is, I weep no tears.

American democracy, my entire life, goes down the drain . . .
For the ruin of that democracy let Sam Gompers sustain no
    blame . . .

He goes out, one or two of the BOSSES *trying to catch him up and talk to
him, almost pleadingly. Exeunt all.*

SCENE 7

Enter LILLIE *with a bundle of clothes. She is heavy with child.*

Lillie   *I* know: but *he* does not know yet

> The word already has gone out
> He's lost his job for what he did
> With his word and banner at the factory gate.
> And I myself am almost brought to bed
> With his seventh child, much sooner than I thought.
> Nora!

Enter NORA.

Do you suppose, child, you will be able to take over my piece-work, and go to school – at least in the mornings – and also make sure that your father gets his food and your brother and sisters get theirs, and that they all go to sleep at the right time of night, and above all that he doesn't discover how much work you are doing when his back's turned?

Nora I don't see why not, Mammy. He spends half his time in New York now, fixing up his arrangements with the IWW – whenever they don't need him at Singers in fact, he's needed three times over at the Wobbly headquarters.

Lillie Whenever they don't need him at Singers will be *every* day from now on: and its best you should know it at once. So even when the baby's born and I'm able to be about again, we are still going to need your two hands: do you understand that? It's a heavy responsibility for one so young. Can you deal with it?

Nora So many of the girls in my school already deal with it: and besides aren't they always telling me the Irish are good for nothing but work!

Lillie   Nothing but work and the breeding of children
> Till the ache of the one of 'em's given way to the pain
> Of the other: and the time has arrived once again:
> So they've sent for my husband, they have sent for the doctor . . .
> While I lie down and fight by myself in my bedroom alone:
> Let them come, let them run . . .

She goes out, followed by NORA *in a panic, dropping clothes everywhere. A pause. Enter* SUPERVISOR.

Supervisor (*knocks*) Hello there – Jim Connolly – anyone at home – ?

Re-enter NORA.

Nora Oh Doctor, is that you – thank heavens you got the message – oh.

Supervisor Say, I'm not no doctor – you expecting him, what's wrong? Look, I guess it's a bad time, honey, if somebody's sick in the house – but I gotta talk to your father, it's only for a moment –

Enter CONNOLLY.

Connolly Nora, where are you? I came as fast as I could! Has the doctor been sent for? Where's your mother – is she in bed?

Nora She's upstairs and everything's ready, and Ina ran round for the doctor:

we had everything laid out the way we were told to and I don't think we forgot anything – oh.

Connolly (*follows her look and realises* SUPERVISOR *is standing there*) Oh. Not just now: I can't deal with it just now.

Supervisor I won't be one moment but I gotta put it to you straight just what Schmidtkopf told me –

Nora Here's the doctor now!

She lets the DOCTOR *in.*

Connolly Thank God. Dr Rosen, she's gone into labour, now I think everything's ready. I'm not without experience –

Doctor Hot water?

Nora In the kitchen, Doctor –

Doctor Towels, napkins, clean sheets –

Nora They're all on the fender in front of the kitchen stove –

Doctor Fine, that's just fine – you got a grand little nurse on the premises, that's one thing, Mr Connolly –

Exit at opposite side.

Connolly What on earth is all this clutter? You should have had the whole house tidy for an occasion like this . . . Never mind, never mind, dear: I'll sort it away myself . . . Dear me, I had no idea I had this many shirts and collars . . .

Supervisor I guess I'd better go and come back in –

Connolly In the morning?

Supervisor – in an hour or two – it *is* urgent.

Connolly I'm *not* having you round here in the next two hours, that's flat. Tell me what you came to tell and for Godsake get it over with!

Supervisor Okay: so when Schmidtkopf came and told me he was putting you in my machine-shop, I told him after one day that sure as hell your qualifications were as phoney as a bald hairdresser. I clamped my teeth and *accepted* you, just the same I had to do for two-thirds of all the others. But when they asked me last month to put forward a good man's name for a replacement for Joe Lambrini, goddammit, I gave 'em yours!

Connolly You did? That was very generous –

Supervisor I tell you they are making shit-pies out of Schmidtkopf – permitting, indeed condoning red revolutionary anarchism to be preached at their very gates, so where the hell does that leave *me*!

Doctor (*briefly reappears*) Mr Connolly – the hot water –

Connolly (*to* SUPERVISOR) Just a moment –

Nora It's all right, I've already got it –

Connolly (*sudden panic*) Nora, come back here – you are not to touch that kettle!

But she has already carried it past him. He turns back to the SUPERVISOR.

I defy either you or Schmidtkopf to prove I have done more than recommend a few workers to consider joining a labour union –

Supervisor So lookit, Jim, I worked for Singers for twenty-five years, my wife
for the past five years is sick, crippled with the arthritis, we got one
grown-up daughter has lived in an institution since eighteen hundred
and ninety-five on account as you know she has got this disability . . .
Jim, if I lose my place in Singers, what in hell am I gonna do?

Connolly If Singers was a union shop these questions would never arise.

Supervisor I ain't got nuth'n against the unions – I want only to keep my job.

Connolly (*after a moment's thought*) Okay: for you: I will quit.

Supervisor But – but where will you go?

Connolly I have a class of a possibility of a political job in New York – an
organiser for the IWW.

Supervisor They would *pay* you for that?

CONNOLLY *shrugs.*

Crazy, goddam crazy – oh hell, I've gotta tell you, I feel very bad about
this – here you take this –

He offers money.

No, don't you look at it. In your pocket. I insist. And keep your goddam
mouth shut. And if anyone in the plant asks me should he join with a
union, I will tell him yes he should, and to tell everyone else that's
exactly what they should all do – *all* of them, goddammit!

Connolly Oh shut up and get out and let me wait for the baby!

The SUPERVISOR *looks as if he would say something else, but thinks better
of it, shakes* CONNOLLY *by the hand, and exits.*

CONNOLLY *waits in silence. A rush of feet. Enter* NORA.

Nora Daddy daddy daddy – !

Enter DOCTOR.

Doctor Mr Connolly, congratulations. A little girl, sir, in very good shape,
and Mrs Connolly as well, sir, fine spirits, excellent shape . . .! I've given
her a sedative, you are not to go upstairs for another two hours at least.

Exit. CONNOLLY *starts rummaging for something.*

Nora Daddy, what are you looking for?

Connolly The manuscript of the history of Irish Labour I was writing – I
thought maybe for an hour or two, if you wouldn't mind helping me –
there's a chapter I'd like to hear you read over to me for correction.

Nora It's in the other room.

Connolly Then we go to the other room! And for heaven's sake leave your
friends to do their own sewing for once!

He gives her a big hug and exeunt.

SCENE 8

Enter ELIZABETH GURLEY FLYNN, *the* IRISH PARTY WORKER *from Scene 5, and a crowd of Irish-Americans (including a* PUBLICAN *and an* OLD FENIAN*). A banner in green, reading 'Irish Socialist Federation (New York) – "Faugh-a-Ballach"*', *is unfurled at the back. Irish music, dancing, conviviality.*

Flynn To every group of immigrants who arrive on these shores there needs to be made available their own socialist club, where, through a course of comprehensive political education, they can eventually find their way into the mainstream of the Socialist Labor Party.

Party Worker (*sings*)
> Now all our people can learn at last
> Home Rule is not the cure for the nation
> But a sound republican line laid down
> By the Irish Socialist Federation.

Enter CONNOLLY *and leads the chorus.*

Connolly (*sings with the crowd*)
> Giddy-i-ay from the USA
> Giddy-i-ay we'll send it homeward
> Giddy-i-ay we'll bear in mind
> The future of our native land!

Flynn (*sings*)
> Or else we know they will all too soon
> Fall prey to Tammany graft and corruption:
> The political boss, the commercial boss
> Outvie one another in exploitation.

Connolly and others (*sing*)
> Giddy-i-ay the New York Irish
> Giddy-i-ay are fleeced and cheated
> Giddy-i-ay in the sacred name
> Of Freedom for our Native Land!

Connolly We have a programme of lectures and discussions – the leaflets are available over there – I intend when funds are sufficient to start our own newspaper – No political group, however modest its intention, can ever do anything without some sort of news-sheet – and our intention is *not* modest. Nothing less than the complete liberation of Ireland and the establishment therein of a socialist republic! I am already in contact with a number of old colleagues of the movement back in Dublin – ideally our newspaper should be a transatlantic publication: but as to that we shall have to see. I thought we might call it *The Harp*. Any opinions?

Publican (*who has not really been listening until this moment*) And by the same token, more power to you, boy! Say, feller, I don't know your name – Connaughton, O'Conroy – ?

Connolly Connolly.

Publican So put it there, Connolly: you're a little guy, but you're a man! *The Harp*! Yeah – swell – 'The Harp that once through Tara's halls . . .' Say, you tell me you need funds? I'm Slattery. Shaun Slattery from Sallynoggin, Sallynoggin County Dublin: and of Slattery's Irish Bar, one hundred and seventy-nine East Eleventh Street, New York! I'm over here forty years – and I made it and I made it good! You want freedom for the ould country? Shaun Slattery will stake you out!

He ladles money out of his pockets and thrusts it into CONNOLLY'*s hands.*

For a newspaper, you need capital, you need investors, you need advertisers – and in this city you need protection! No better man than Slattery! – Chief ward-boss for the Democrats five blocks around East Eleventh Street – ask any man down Second Avenue: where stands Slattery? And he'll answer: 'If Slattery is not on his knees in the confessional: then look for the bould Shaun among the wheel-and-deal of City Hall!'

Connolly I wonder, Mr Slattery, did you altogether hear my programme?

Publican Is it socialism? Sure aren't all the Irish socialists, when it comes to denouncing th'brutal tyranny of th'crown of Britain? But these two things I have no time for: that's atheism and protestants. The day we get Home Rule and a Dublin parliament of our own, we'll drive the pack of 'em into the sea like St Patrick with the snakes!

Connolly (*to* PARTY WORKER) Jack, get rid of him.

Publican Wh – what – ?

Connolly Trying to buy *me* with your wheeling-dealing dollars – get out of here, you parasite, before I forget meself!

A Guest Mr Connolly, it's not wise to be having trouble with Mr Slattery . . .

Publican (*on his way out*) We'll not forget this, Connolly! You'll be marked for it, I'm tellin' you! I know men in this town who are *killers*: they're in my pocket!

The PARTY WORKER *expels him. The* OLD FENIAN *takes* CONNOLLY *aside.*

Old Fenian He means the police.

Connolly I don't care if he means the state governor and the president all rolled up into one!

Old Fenian Sure he has New York's Finest bought-and-sold, there's no doubt. But I don't think you'll be hearing from them. Sure I know the man well. Sixty-seven indeed he did come over here, 'tis true, but whereas some of us were accredited rebels in the insurrection of that year, there was more than a suspicion your man Slattery was an *informer*: he knows that I know it: I don't think you'll have trouble. Oh he keeps very quiet where the Brotherhood is in question. Did you know, Mr Connolly, that the

Irish Republican Brotherhood, or the Fenians, as it was then, had close ties with the Revolutionary Socialist International that began in Europe in forty-eight?

Connolly I had heard it, sir, yes. My uncle was involved in the business of sixty-seven. MacBride was the name he adopted.

Old Fenian I know it well: we checked it out. We're very interested in your programme. I wonder if I could take a moment, while our friends are at the revels, to put down a few feelers to judge what yourself would be thinking of ours?

Connolly I am not thinking of anything beyond public organisation for a defined political goal. Conspiracy is not my angle.

Old Fenian There's no denying that in the underground side of the business we do have to rub up against a few you'd find abhorrent. One day, don't you know, you too may be in search of a very similar class of 'parasite'. If you need a man to put you on to them, don't you be looking any further than me. I have a feeling, don't you know, that 'one day' could be quite soon. . . . Good luck to you, so: I'll take occasion to purchase a pile of your literature . . .

DE LEON *has come quietly up to them, having bought one or two of the pamphlets.*

De Leon Comrade Connolly – no – don't disturb yourself. I was just passing through and I thought I should drop in to congratulate you on your achievement – on being elected, I mean, by the New Jersey SLP, to the National Executive Committee of the party. A product of your herculean efforts in the Haywood-Moyer defence campaign? And this, I suppose –

Holds up one of the pamphlets.

– a product of your energetic pen? 'Socialism and Religion – the known and the unknowable' . . . unknowable indeed . . . I met a certain influential local Democrat on his way out: he seemed annoyed?

Connolly He was.

De Leon Good. Might it not have been better had you avoided involving his emotions in either direction? I never find him on the threshold of any of *my* meetings, Comrade Connolly . . . Oh by the way, here is an advance copy of tomorrow's *Weekly People*. You might care to take a look at it?

Exit.

Flynn What did he give you that for?

Connolly There must be something in it of a *correctional* nature . . . by God there is! Stromqvist, from Arizona. Writes a letter denouncing the whole idea of socialist federations within ethnic communities. We must answer it.

Party Worker How?

Connolly With a firm argument. It is impossible for poor immigrants to re-
linquish all at once their foreign roots in favour of a strange abstract
doctrine. Make it clear to the silly man that it's time he had some
humanity.

Party Worker De Leon won't like it.

Flynn I sometimes get the idea we all came here in the first place to drive De
Leon into the looney-bin.

Connolly Lizzie, I do believe he really believes that. At all points I seem to
find myself attacking his centralisation of power: and yet God knows, I
do stand fast, very fast indeed, for a well-organised disciplined party.
Sure, what could I not have done with one, had I had it in Dublin? At
all events I intend to keep quiet as a mouse on the National Executive
Committee. No, I'll not give them a fingerhold to raise one single
objection to me. . . .

Exeunt.

SCENE 9

A scene in the dark. VOICES OF NEWSBOYS.

1st Voice Big Bill Haywood acquitted! Jury find no evidence for labour
leader's involvement in Idaho conspiracy!

2nd Voice Jury verdict in Idaho pins guilt for frame-up on Pinkerton Detective
Agency!

HAYWOOD *appears in spotlight, as just released, amidst cheers.* MOYER *and*
PETTIBONE *beside him.*

1st Voice Brother Haywood, have you a few words for the Socialist Party
newspaper, *Appeal to Reason*?

2nd Voice Comrade, the Socialist Labor Party's *Weekly People* would be glad
of an interview!

3rd Voice *The American Federationist*, house organ of the AF of L, wants to
ask a few questions . . .

Haywood I'm out and I'm proven innocent and I'm back in circulation: they
tried to break the Miners' Union and they tried to break the Wobblies,
but instead we broke *them* – and brothers, the class war goes on from this
regardless! Unabated!

3rd Voice Bill, is it true that Charlie Moyer and yourself are no longer such
good friends?

Haywood I don't want to say nothing against my old pardner Charlie Moyer.
I hold my views as I always did and you all know what they are. About
his views, you should ask him.

3rd Voice Say, Charlie, is it true that a majority of the Western Miners aim
to pull out of the IWW and they're asking for your leadership?

Moyer My opinion the time has come to return to a moderate and practicable basis of day-to-day trade union business and to quit playing cowboys-and-injuns with the livelihoods of working men.

HAYWOOD *and* MOYER *move ostentatiously apart.*

2nd Voice We haven't heard from Comrade Pettibone –
1st Voice Brother Pettibone, what's your angle?
Pettibone It was all a mistake. I was never in no radical plot: I was never no more than a sympathiser with the union. I got sick inside of jail. I got myself real sick. Guess I wanna go home and just talk no more about it . . .

He goes out.

Haywood Through national working-class solidarity alone we stand here free tonight: I appeal to the whole movement throughout America not to break that solidarity!
Moyer No, we gotta see somehow this kinda thing never happens again: we gotta keep our heads clear, we gotta . . .

HAYWOOD *stalks away and out in disgust.* GOMPERS *is revealed coming up to* MOYER *and putting an arm round his shoulder.*

Gompers We gotta get them Western Miners re-organised now on a totally new system of the best thing for the most members at this one point of time. Charlie: you got no option – in the AF of L, or nowhere!
Moyer In the AF of L. . . .

GOMPERS *takes him out, protective and paternal.*

Haywood (*calls from the shadows*) The class war goes on regardless: regardless and unabated!

Lights up, stage empty.

SCENE 10

Enter CONNOLLY.

Connolly Oh yes, I have risen up, I am now tall, I am a marvellous man; I am elected, no less, to the National Executive Committee of the Socialist Labor Party – and I'm supposed to have turned docile. Oh I've said nothing yet – at least not much – at least just a few headings jotted down as to what's wrong with the entire party and why Dan De Leon with his arrogant exclusivism leads us all into the wilderness . . . ! I began, very modestly, at my first major meeting of the National Executive Committee, by asking my fellow-delegates what exactly they conceived to be the overall role of the newspaper . . .

Enter DE LEON, *separate from* CONNOLLY, *at another corner. The two address the audience alternately, without overt reference to one another.*

De Leon As it happens I was not present at this particular meeting. I had a
prior engagement – –

Connolly Lounging on the beach at Miami, it was rumoured – –

De Leon Addressing a university seminar at Yale upon international economic trends.

Connolly At all events, I had discovered that a hard-working party group – the
New York executive sub-committee, to be precise – had had notice of
their resolutions published as of right in *The Weekly People*. Now, it so
happened, in this case, that one particular resolution had for some
reason caused De Leon a certain amount of annoyance.

De Leon The resolution of the sub-committee had completely misrepresented
the position of the party on the matter of the supply of funds to overseas
socialist groups! In the newspaper such an indiscretion would be taken
all over the world as evidence that my policy had radically changed! 'For
some reason' indeed – it was an issue of the utmost importance – I made
it clear that the sub-committee from now on had no right to insert its
half-baked notions into the official party organ.

Connolly I wanted it made clear that the role of these sub-committees could
only come to its necessary fruition within the party if they were allowed
full scope to express their activities in the newspaper. So I put down a
motion. I knew De Leon's creatures would of course all be against me,
and that if the motion had been worded: 'The National Executive Committee considers that the sub-committee has the right to insert official
matter in the *People*' then automatically it would be rejected and nothing
more would be said. No: I needed to make certain that even if it were
rejected, it could only be rejected after a very full and wide discussion.
Dammit, it was more than time that *somebody* discussed the central
oligarchy of the party and the . . . the dictatorship that they imposed!
So I played it crafty – –

De Leon The classic technique of the professional wrecker! Sowing confusion
and disunity with deliberate ambiguous tricks!

Connolly I worded my motion thus: 'This committee considers that the
National Executive Committee *and* its sub-committee have the right to
insert official matter in *The People*'. D'you get it? The National Executive
Committee, the NEC, that's *us* – we already had the right: it was only
the sub-committee had had their right taken away. I made it an issue it
was *both* committees or nothing. They couldn't reject the right of the
sub-committee without rejecting the right of the NEC as well – the only
way they could get out of it was by proposing amendments: and if they'd
done that, they'd have given me just exactly what I wanted: a full and
wide discussion of the whole business of central control! But d'ye know,
they didn't do it! The bloody eedjits couldn't see one single implication
of – –

De Leon Please take note all this went on when I myself was not present –
addressing a university seminar at Yale upon – –

Connolly The bloody eedjits could see nothing but that James Connolly had put a motion down. The word was out that any nonsense emanating from the man Connolly was automatically to be opposed. Without an iota of reasoned argument they voted against me *en bloc*: just like that! And the result is –

De Leon The result is that the National Executive Committee – *my* committee – the policy-making body of the foremost revolutionary force in the entire western hemisphere – has been manipulated into denying itself access to its own newspaper!

Exit.

Connolly So what in the devil's name are they going to do next? Would they honourably admit they had made a mistake: go back over the whole question? How could they? Because if they did, they would have to grant me the full and wide discussion I had intended in the first place. So I expected some small deviousness. I was prepared for it. I wrote out statements . . . In my wildest dreams I never thought that they would refuse to accept my statements, that the columns of the newspaper would be closed to me absolutely, that an irregular meeting of the NEC would be held when I was not present – deliberately so held . . . and that all I could do against them was to wearily write out copy after copy of my personal deposition and circulate it by hand to individual party-members . . . three-quarters of them never even bothered to acknowledge it. Oh what's the use . . .

Exit.

SCENE 11

Enter DE LEON *and Socialist Labor Party* OFFICIALS.

De Leon (*as they take their seats*) Comrades, if you please, just take it easy, one and all . . . As you know, I was not at the NEC meeting when this ridiculous Connolly motion was put forward and misunderstood. I have only the minutes of the meeting to go on: but it seems to me quite incredible that a caucus of intelligent socialists could take a vote on they know not what.

1st Official The fact remains, Comrade De Leon, we have gotten ourselves entangled into a position of unresolved deadlock. If we – –

De Leon If we allow ourselves to get rattled we will only make it worse. Comrade Zimmerman, you've always been a pretty cool customer, I guess. What did *you* think you were voting against? Speak carefully. Take your time.

2nd Official (*as though repeating lines learnt by rote*) I believed, Comrade De Leon, that the motion had reference alone to the . . .

De Leon To the . . . ?

2nd Official To the sub-committee, and nothing else.

De Leon Hah. And it was only when you – ?

2nd Official It was only when I saw the minutes several days later that I knew there had been a – –

De Leon So if your well-trained analytical memory is contradicted by the minutes, then in all probability, the minutes are incorrect. Comrade Secretary?

Secretary I don't know . . . I could swear, comrade, I got it right . . . According to my typescript . . .

De Leon We know what's on your typescript. But what about your original pencilled notes?

Secretary I don't have them any more. I threw them away, I guess . . .

De Leon I guess therefore we assume that the motion referred only to the sub-committee, that the mention of both committees got into the minutes in error: and that the minutes will accordingly be amended to comply with the – with the collective memory of those present.

3rd Official Comrade, may I point out that those present do not include Comrade Connolly himself? If he is not here when his own business is being discussed – –

De Leon Was *I* here when *my* business as editor of the newspaper was discussed at the last meeting? Comrade Connolly had every warning that his activities were to be investigated: if he has chosen to absent himself, he has done so in a petulant and non-co-operative spirit: he must therefore take the consequences! Amend the minutes.

Secretary (*does so*) 'Motion before the meeting: "This committee considers that the NEC sub-committee has the right to insert official matter in *The People*." Motion rejected.' Is that right?

De Leon Of course one can see how easily the mistake arose. 'The NEC sub-committee' . . . a smudge on our good friend's notebook led him to transcribe it as 'the NEC *and its* sub-committee' . . . well, we're all of us fallible. Be more vigilant in future, please. Next business?

Secretary A letter from Comrade Connolly, offering his resignation from the National Executive Committee.

De Leon I see. Comrade Zimmerman?

2nd Official (*as though prompted*) May I move a resolution that this committee reject Comrade Connolly's resignation until he has first appeared in person before us to receive censure for his provocative conduct: and if it is decided that this committee would be better off without him, he be expelled herefrom with ignominy.

1st Official I second that.

3rd Official And I oppose it! Comrade Connolly has been the object of an unscrupulous and vindictive personal campaign – –

De Leon Comrade, these individualist petty-bourgeois outbursts are scarcely compatible with our revolutionary task! How can you say 'personal'

when you consider the social background of an Irishman of this type?
At what college was he educated?

3rd Official I don't know the sort of colleges are available in Ireland . . .

De Leon Well, *I* do. Clerical seminaries: and the best of them Jesuit! Oh my
own family lived in just such a society – we were Sephardic Jews, if you
please, in Spanish America – we knew all about the Jesuits, pursuing
their secret mission till the whole world has been subverted to the grand
design of the church of Rome! If James Connolly is not an undercover
Jesuit, the only other thing he could be is a complete and blundering
idiot. I have read too much of his literature to believe that: far too
much . . . I call the meeting to order. Votes? . . . The resolution is carried
by a substantial majority. Thank you, comrades: good-night.

He gets up and goes. The others follow.

SCENE 12

Enter GOMPERS *and* GRABITALL. *An* AFL OFFICIAL *in the background.*

Grabitall I thought you told me the AF of L had taken over the Western
Miners!

Gompers Work in progress . . . procedural hold-ups . . . maybe next year all
the deals will be finalised . . . how can I tell?

Grabitall There is a *strike*!

Gompers Sure there's a strike. In this business, mister, there's nuth'n but
goddam strikes . . .

Grabitall At Goldfield, Nevada: the Federation of Western Miners in cahoots
with the IWW – I thought you told me – –

Gompers You think you can break that strike?

Grabitall The state militia has been sent in! We have martial law proclaimed
all over the – –

Gompers So maybe then you'll break it: so maybe then the Western Miners
and the IWW will speed up their split: so maybe procedural hang-ups
will be liquidised before next year. Mister, you just relax. Sam Gompers
knows his onions.

Grabitall What instructions have been given your AFL locals in the area of
Goldfield?

Gompers To pass the pickets, what else? Are you satisfied?

Grabitall I am not! I'd have you know that the mining company is bankrupt!

Gompers That's your problem. Glad to have met you.

He turns abruptly away. Baffled, GRABITALL *goes out.*

Official In Goldfield *we* got problems. Our carpenters in the mines have cut
up rough about the militia. They don't want to pass the pickets: there's
been words heard like 'betrayal'.

Gompers In my outfit! Such delusions! My integrity was never better.

Enter 2ND OFFICIAL *and a* PEACE-OFFICER.

2nd Official Hey, boss, there's a pig here, come to *arrest* you! What'll we do?

Gompers Arrest? Okay, I'm a martyr. Tell me the charge.

Peace-Officer Contempt of court. Your newspaper *The American Federationist* defamed the Stove and Range Company of St Louis Missouri in connection with a strike. You was injuncted by the court to refrain from interference. You defied the injunction. You're awarded six months inside.

Gompers (*holds out hands for manacles*) Didn't I tell you my integrity was never better? Lead the way.

Exeunt.

SCENE 13

Enter CONNOLLY.

Connolly I need not explain I did not in person present myself to De Leon's committee to be censured, expelled with ignominy! Instead I did succeed in securing myself a paid appointment – Building Section (New York) Organiser of the Industrial Workers of the World! And I brought the family there to live, in a deplorable Bronx apartment, and the Irish Socialist Federation has its headquarters just round the corner . . . it's as though I have been reborn into a whole new phase of American life . . . !

Sings and dances.

> With De Leon and his party I am finished and done:
> For all of four years I played his tune
> On a broken-backed fiddle with the strings all gone –
> And I danced like a dervish in a dumb dark room
> With a carpet on the wall and cork on the floor
> And wood across the window and a nailed-up door!

And now thank God I've busted out of it: I am my own man at last, can activate and organise in full liberty to my heart's content: and, merciful hour, they pay me *money* for it!

> Poor old Dan, determined man,
> The only bloody socialist in God's own land!
> And when in the end revolution comes
> He'll be there in his kitchen just a pile of old bones.
> The people will march and the bones will stir—
> But who will hear them knocking on the floor?
>
> The statue of liberty will loose her hair
> And toss her crown into the air,

Unbuckle her gown and let it fall
And jump into the harbour like a great white whale!
Who is it will swim astride her limbs
But those whom dead old Dan condemns?

Free in the air and free in the water
Watch us sport with liberty's daughter –
Sport and swim, good-bye to him –
His fiddle is broke but trumpet-and-drum,
The jews'-harp, the spoons and the cute banjo
Will rattle up a tune and away we go . . .
Tum ta-ta ra-rah – tum-tum . . . !

*Exit, dancing, and waving an IWW banner, followed by a surge of Wobbly
demonstrators in great excitement.*

END OF ACT 2

ACT 3: Forward to the Revolution...?

SCENE 1

Immigrants arriving in the USA from a ship; with the Statue of Liberty, watchful police, and skyscrapers filling the background, so that little or on sky is visible (Backcloth 6.)

The wide open spaces of America, mountain, desert and farmland, with groups of workers with red flags confronting armed posses of sheriffs' deputies, Ku Klux Klan etc. (Backcloth 7.)

A breadline of UNEMPLOYED *with a placard: '1907 – Slump Hits USA – Five Million Out of Work!'*

At the other side, CONNOLLY *and* LILLIE *– he in bed, she sitting with a candle, sewing. Atmosphere of intense cold.*

Unemployed (*sing*)
    I don't want your millions, mister:
    I don't want your diamond ring.
    All I want is the right to live, mister:
    Give me my job back again.

Connolly (*unable to sleep, stirs, sits up*) Five million. So cold, cold. Freeze to death on the streets at night. They told me at the Pennsylvania Station that a train came in from Baltimore with three hoboes frozen fast to the rods under the coaches, with crowbars they had to break their arms and legs from the iron. One of them with the small pink card in the heel of his sock. He'd have come to see me if he'd lived. Could be that he'd come to New York for no other purpose but to come to see me. District organiser, Industrial Workers of the World – what in hell could I have done for him?

Lillie James, why don't you roll over and go back to sleep – you have to be down at Hoboken tomorrow morning for that open-air meeting.

Connolly Twelve thousand waterside workers will be voting to enter the IWW en bloc. It could be the biggest thing for us since – –

Lillie Half-past six by torchlight, in the cold wind of the waterfront – James, you could get pneumonia: do, please, have some sleep first!

Connolly The American Federation of Labor put out the bids for 'em, but no, their leaders said 'it's the new union or nothing!' We must have that mass membership – it could be the one thing to save us in New York ... Lillie, what the devil are you doing, girl! Leave your sewing till to-morrow or you'll make yourself ill.

Lillie I've only got another twenty of these bodices to finish – I'll come to bed then, I promise – but, James, it's a rush job and Mr Shapiro insisted that – –

Connolly You don't have to do it! I am paid by the union, Lillie, you do not have to make a slave of yourself in this way.

Lillie Last week you were paid. But next week? You can guarantee it? Shapiro can guarantee it. He's a man of his word.

Connolly How can he be, he's a damn slave-driver: he makes you into the slave of a slave: for me and the children you have to – –

Lillie James: you have your job and it's the only job you want to do. So please let me do mine: and then the children can be fed. Nora already earned six dollars this week in that dressmaking house: if I can bring in four, with your eighteen that makes – –

Connolly Does it make enough to pay the plumber to fix the frozen pipe, will you tell me?

Lillie Will you pass me the red cotton? Now turn over and go to sleep.

Unemployed (*sing*)

We worked to build this country, mister
While you enjoyed a life of ease:
You've stolen all that we built, mister:
Now our children starve and freeze.

Connolly (*checks through his notebooks*) Building and Construction Workers' Section, local ninety-five. Good. Steel-erectors . . . bronze-workers . . . carpenters . . . good. Brooklyn local number fourteen. Not so good. Plasterers in difficulty with the AF of L. There's a new local for their craft-workers on the site of the warehouse project. They made trouble on the job. Donovan told me the AF of L sent delegates down to the site . . .

INTERLUDE 1. *Enter* FOREMAN *and* BUILDING WORKERS: *to them an* AF OF L OFFICIAL. HOODLUMS *enter behind.*

AF of L Official You the foreman here? You got non-union labour on this site, that correct?

Foreman This ain't no closed shop, mister – –

AF of L Official From now on as far as the plasterers is concerned that's exactly what it is, mac – which of you guys holds a union card? Show! Okay . . . okay . . . Who are you, you ain't got nuth'n, stand aside . . . What the hell's this?

1st Worker That's what they call the little pink card, friend – IWW –

AF of L Official Since when was the IWW a Plasterers' Union?

1st Worker It's a Construction Union, fair and square – we pay our dues, we –

AF of L Official You swallow up the employment of skilled men like it was oatmeal porridge, you damned Wobbly! Construction Union my ass – crowd of conniving scabs. Here we are, boys, he's a Wobbly – get him off!

HOODLUMS *beat up* 1ST WORKER *and throw him out.*

You, without a card: you have the choice to follow him or apply for probationary membership of the Plasterers' Union, AF of L. Which?

2nd Worker I'll apply.

AF of L Official There's a fee for examination of your skill of three dollars.

2ND WORKER *hands it over.* AF OF L OFFICIAL *gives one dollar to* FOREMAN.

From now on, that's the arrangement, get it? Sorry for the trouble, but as you see the AF of L members refuse outright to work with Wobblies. Remember that, next man you hire – okay?

Exeunt. (*Throughout these sequences,* CONNOLLY *and* LILLIE *remain.*)

Connolly Only way we can break the stranglehold of the AF of L is to recruit and recruit new members from all over. The IWW Propaganda League has nothing but that for its object, but in this city – so vast, so contorted an ice-bound labyrinth – how in the name of God to get hold of the men? We do not even have any premises for our meeting . . .

INTERLUDE 2. *Re-enter* AF *of* L OFFICIAL, *with his* HOODLUMS. *They prevent* WORKERS *from passing into an IWW meeting.*

AF of L Official The vote taken by this local of an AF of L Union for provision of premises for the IWW was overruled on account of irregularity, get it? If you aint got no hall of your own for your meetings, that's your funeral. Move! For anarchists and red subversives we got no provision in our rule-book – Sam Gompers is a loyal American.

Enter GOMPERS.

Gompers To keep the American Federation of Labor, in this time of depression, uncontaminated by those who seek only to destroy the entire fabric of our democracy, is a task of the first importance. The IWW is deliberately encouraging an uncontrolled flood of unskilled revolutionary immigrants to pour into this country to lay hands on the prosperity American workers have amassed through generations of patient toil. They gotta be stopped – be stopped right now.

Exit, with AF OF L OFFICIAL *and* HOODLUMS.

Connolly Unskilled revolutionary immigrants . . . ha . . . ! Are the Irish revolutionary . . . ? Oh rebels, aye aye, no doubt about that, and when we come in to this country: against Britain; against imperialism every man of us is a Dan O'Connell: and so enchanted with our own verbiage we drift in a dream of whiskey through the portals of Tammany Hall.

INTERLUDE 3.

Irish Immigrant (*sings*)
> I'm a decent boy just landed from the town of Ballyfad,
> I want a situation and I want it very bad:
> I have seen employment advertised, 'It's just the thing,' says I –
> But the dirty spalpeen ended with 'No Irish need apply.'

'Whoo' says I, 'That's an insult but to get the place I'll try';
So I went to see the blackguard with his 'No Irish need apply'.
Some do think it a misfortune to be christened Pat or Dan
But to me it is an honour to be born an Irishman . . .

Enter Irish-American PUBLICAN.

Publican (*greets* IMMIGRANTS) Shaun Slattery of Slattery's Irish Bar, East
Eleventh Street is your man for every wrinkle to get around the likes of
that. Come in with you, boys, and drink your fill, sure Slattery pays every
round, 'tis on the house for the sake of your arrival in the land of liberty.
Now I'll tell you what it is, boys, next year is the election-year, and the
Democrat Party needs all hands to turn out and bring in again in triumph
the good ould cause – do you tell me you don't know what our candidate
has promised? The word must be bloody slow then getting back to the
Ring of Kerry! Have ye never heard of the congressional resolution
demanding be all means short of war that the King of England packs his
bags and quits Ireland on the double? Sure 'tis only for the backing of
the Democratic lobby here that the Home Rulers in Westminster have it
going for them at all at all . . . Now there's five dollars a man from the
hand of Slattery if the Republican meeting at Cooper Union tomorrow
night should be accidentally cut to ribbons be an unacknowledged ele-
ment inserted in amongst the crowd – sure the police have all been
squared . . . And let me tell you, boys, any man here having trouble with
his accommodations or his taxes or his eventual American citizenship
has only to put the word out and the bould Slattery will come running . . .
There you are then, and you after thinking there was no good for you at
all in the streets of New York . . . And when the Cardinal Archbishop of
Armagh pays his visit here at the end of next week, wouldn't we all be
keen to render him the full honours of our new country . . . ?

The IMMIGRANT *crowd accept his munificence with due respect and
gratitude.*

INTERLUDE 4. *Enter the* CARDINAL, *as though for a press conference,
managed by the* PUBLICAN. ELIZABETH GURLEY FLYNN *is among the crowd.*

Cardinal My visit to America of course is primarily a spiritual mission: the
faith of the Irish is justly celebrated throughout America as the backbone
of the Catholic Church – but I agreed to meet the press today in the ex-
pectation that perhaps a few more worldly matters might be of interest
to some Americans . . . yes?

A Reporter (*from the back*) Your Eminence, do you consider that Congress
should put pressure on Great Britain to introduce Home Rule for
Ireland?

Cardinal The Irish National Home Rule Party seeks the fullest Irish autonomy
consistent with the unity of the British Empire and I am unequivocal in
lending my support to that – ah – most justified aspiration . . . yes?

Reporter Your Eminence, would you consider that, given Home Rule, there would be scope for American business to invest in Irish industry?

Cardinal Irish industry already is a flourishing child – but she will need the most sympathetic help if she is to be reared to that status fully commensurate with – ah – maturity . . . yes?

Flynn (*also from the back*) I wonder would His Eminence care to comment on how Home Rule might mend the condition of the working class in Dublin, where the housing is notorious as by far the worst in Europe and where –

Cardinal Ah, now as to housing – Mr Slattery, what newspaper does this lady represent?

Flynn *The Harp* – official organ of the Irish Socialist Federation!

Connolly Oh Lizzie, well done, Lizzie, but she didn't get too far with it – oh dear . . .

Publican Begod, that's the atheistical rag that lowdown louser of a Connolly edits up hill and down dale! Let the stewards at the back there control the disturbance now! Aye aye have her out of it!

ELIZABETH GURLEY FLYNN *is thrown out.*

Cardinal Let me say about socialism – this importation from the continent of Europe – that it denies the existence of God, the immortality of the soul, the right of private ownership, the rightful existence of our present social organisation, and the independence of the church as a society complete in itself and founded by God.

Publican True for you, Your Eminence – didn't Father Sherman S.J. make an echo of your very voice when he told us last month that the socialists are nothing else than hell's lowest vomit? And didn't the Bishop of – –

Cardinal I am not here however to interfere in any way with the American political process . . .

Exeunt CARDINAL *and* PUBLICAN.

Connolly God in Heaven! What wonder that the immigrants from the bog and mountain are such material for scabs and blacklegs, the foul lies they have been choked with before even they reach these shores!

He strides about in agitation. Abruptly changes the subject:

Lillie – I never asked you what you thought of the motto we have posted on the front page of *The Harp*? 'In things essential, unity: in things doubtful, diversity: in all things, charity'?

Lillie For a man that's been slung out of the American Socialist Labor Party and was forced to resign from his own party back in Dublin, I'd say that your conception of charity was a little large, James. Yet you still write every week to O'Brien in Dublin: and that old wretch De Leon of the SLP has a great deal of influence in the IWW.

Connolly He helped found it: so why wouldn't he. But as for O'Brien – the boys in Dublin have their own new party now, the Socialist Party of Ireland, and whatever my old hurt, I have no choice but keep in touch with them . . . Lord, I wish I was there now!

Lillie Not even in Dublin was it ever so cold as this. Only five more to finish now . . . and then we must go to bed.

Connolly Aye aye, we have *The Harp* – and most of my foolish pamphlets have a decent circulation – you know I actually earned money from my *Socialism Made Easy* – in Australia moreover! If I can only find time to finish my *Labour in Irish History* – Lillie, if I do that, I will have published a *book*! And to whom else should I dedicate it but you?

Lillie   In Scotland he began, in Ireland carried it on,
In huge America can we together yet reach
The wrecked ship stranded on the golden beach
And make it swim?
I don't know: but I do know that for him
There is no other voyage, therefore my part
In it is marked inevitably on his chart.

James, it's ridiculous to pretend there are no successes for the movement in New York. The garment workers' strike – twenty thousand women all on the streets at once: if that was not the principle of One Big Union, what was it? And our own daughter in it – did she make you proud?

INTERLUDE 5. *Enter* GARMENT WORKERS *including* NORA *with a placard* 'Recognise Garment Union Now! Ban Sweatshop Labor!'

Garment Workers (*sing*)
There once was a Union maid, she never was afraid
Of goons and ginks and company finks and the deputy sheriffs
that made the raid –
She went to the union-hall when a meeting it was called
And when the company boys came round she always stood her
ground:
Oh you can't scare me I'm sticking to the Union
I'm sticking to the Union till the day I die!

Connolly Russians, filled with the spirit of the revolution of nineteen hundred and five, Poles, Jewish, Italian, Irish girls – all of 'em –

Garment Workers We raise our right hands and swear, 'If I turn traitor to the cause I now pledge, may this hand wither from the arm I now raise!'

Nora   Nora, James Connolly's daughter, at the age of sixteen
Knows all of her father's life and understands what it should
mean
To be begotten by a man who will turn the whole world upside-
down.

Exeunt. Enter an IWW OFFICIAL.

IWW Official Jim – where's Jim Connolly – look, Jim, you've to go to

Yonkers! There's trouble at the tramway company – say, they've all come out on strike except the electricians in the AF of L craft union, and none of the others is organised worth one cent. The AF of L have instructed their members to pass the picket-line. The strike committee's solid if we can back their action they'll join the IWW en masse – will you come?

Connolly My God, will I not! Lizzie Flynn can go to Hoboken in my place – just wait till I get my trousers on – Lillie, for God's sake, go to bed!

Lillie But what about you?

He runs out without answering, with the IWW OFFICIAL. *Exit* LILLIE.

SCENE 2

Enter STRIKERS *with a placard: 'Yonkers Tramway Strike: Fair Wage and Eight Hour Day for all Crews Now!'*

Tramway Strikers (*sing*)
> It is we who plowed the prairies; built the cities where they trade
> Dug the mines and built the workshops; endless miles of railroad laid.
> Now we stand outcast and starving mid the wonders that we made
> But the union makes us strong! Solidarity for ever
> For the Union makes us strong!

Enter AF OF L OFFICIAL.

AF of L Official What the hell gives with you guys, why you ain't even *got* a union – now listen, the Teamsters' Union AF of L will give you backing in your grievance: but first you gotta come off strike and pull these pickets: there's good union men in the electricians are withheld by you from work!

Strikers Union men? Scabs!
> The scabs crawl in and the scabs crawl out
> They crawl in under and all about . . . (*etcetera*)

Trouble as SCABS *try to pass picket.* POLICE *break it up. Enter* CONNOLLY.

Connolly Now wait a minute – the IWW undertakes to back this action: but the problem of scabs? There's regular blacklegs, right, brought in to do your work: but they can't do it unless the electricians are providing the power for the trolley-cars, right? So you start with the electricians. Go picket them on their own doorsteps, in the streets where they live and shame them into supporting you. You do that, you won't need to run in trouble with the police. Don't listen to this Judas – he wants nothing better than to sell you out. You have a grievance has gone unsettled for twelve months – you said strike, so then strike, and don't let yourselves be diverted. But watch out for provocation –

AF of L Official I don't know no provocation more likely to lead to trouble than these bums of goddam Wobblies – anarchists, syndicalists, non-negotiators, revolutionists!

(The STRIKERS *jeer him.) A* HOODLUM *enters.* AF OF L OFFICIAL *takes him aside.*

Provocation? They can have it! Where the hell's my man – oh there you are. This morning you're no union employee, you're a scab: so go and scab like you was born to it.

The HOODLUM *pulls a gun and runs in towards the picket.*

Hoodlum I'm demanding police protection to afford me the right to work!
Connolly Stand clear of that man, boys, he's a –
But the HOODLUM *has already tangled with a* STRIKER: *in the fight the gun goes off and the* HOODLUM *falls.* POLICE *are whistled up by the* AF OF L OFFICIAL.
AF of L Official I'm a witness of this, officer: he was shot dead by a dirty Wobbly – case of unprovoked homicide!

The STRIKER *is arrested and taken off. The others are shocked rigid.*

Police Officer As of right now I declare this picket in violation of the state law governing public assembly. Break it up or you're all accessories to the homicide – d'you hear me – break it up! Don't speak to me, you, Connolly, or I'll gun you down right now! You got no mandate with these men.
AF of L Official Membership cards of the Teamsters Union may be obtained from my office on payment of the usual fee. Do what the man says, boys, break it up, these fool Wobblies have ruined everything. But listen, you leave it with me – maybe tomorrow with your bosses I can fix you a fair deal . . .

Exeunt, except CONNOLLY.

Connolly All they ever need to do is to mention revolution and then prove that it means murder. That poor fellow's defence must be seen to at once. And after that, the waterside workers . . .

SCENE 3

Enter ELIZABETH GURLEY FLYNN.

Flynn Jim, I don't know that the waterside workers can get into the outfit at all – De Leon is opposing it at the highest level.
Connolly He's out of his mind, the old idiot, twelve thousand of them, one quarter of all the longshoremen that work in Brooklyn, Manhattan, Hoboken – it's ridiculous – and De Leon lays claim to have done more than any single socialist to build the IWW? Tell me why?

Flynn I don't know why . . .
Connolly We'll put a stop to it – now.

Exeunt.

SCENE 4

Enter DE LEON *and a Socialist Labor Party* OFFICIAL.

De Leon Totally unrealistic padding out of the membership rolls of the IWW by means of these mass-admissions of . . . of what are they? Italians?
SLP Official Italians and Irish –
De Leon Italian and Irish catholics: and why? Look at the name of the organiser who sponsors them! *James Connolly*, who else? Not one of them by any stretch of the imagination can be regarded as even the potential possessor of any sort of socialist doctrine! He aims to swamp the organisation with these reactionary ethnic elements for the sole purpose of ensuring that the Socialist Labor Party is permanently out-voted upon the IWW policy-making committees! Aha, we discover the real reason behind the Connolly gang's promotion of these dubious IWW propaganda leagues he has so assiduously been fostering. Hoho, we discover the occult plot to emasculate the nation-wide movement for which the Socialist Labor Party has heretofore been the sole source of political doctrine! We'll put a stop to this – now! When is the next meeting of the general executive board of the IWW?
SLP Official First week of January, Comrade De Leon – in Chicago.
De Leon Have them hold it in New York! Have it convened as a special emergency tribunal – –
SLP Official There'll be trouble about that. I mean, travelling expenses for delegates.
De Leon Expenses, what expenses? I am prepared at the drop of a hat to travel to Chicago – and back the next day – if thus I can bring with me the essential members of the board! Go get me reservations on the rail-road at once – while you're doing it I'll send a wire to forewarn them of the emergency.

Exeunt.

SCENE 5

Enter CONNOLLY, *shivering with cold, and* ELIZABETH GURLEY FLYNN *is selling his papers in cold, snowy weather.*

Connolly So he wants to create crisis, does he, with his special meeting in New York? Does he not know we have already such a crisis of unemploy-ment and poverty in this city that his sectarian feuds when he brings them here will be pelted from off the pavements? Okay, so it's a crisis.

Lizzie; go tell the committee members that in view of the urgency of the industrial situation here, any meetings of internal import must be got rid of as rapidly as possible – so why the hell wait till January – let's have De Leon's meeting on December the twenty-third and get it over with before christmas. Hurry. I'm not well.

FLYNN *hastens out.*

I've been five years in America, ye'd have thought I could have warned myself a winter's night in New York is by no means the same thing as the same thing in Dublin – like a damnfool I sell newspapers for three hours outside the Cooper Union. Nora – where are you, dear, will you – will you get me my cup o' tea?

Enter NORA *who finds him collapsing.*

Nora Daddy, you must come to bed, you can't go out again to a meeting tonight.

Connolly No, not tonight, but the twenty-third – I'll be fine by the twenty-third – I must have the documents on the waterside workers – will you bring them to the bedroom –

Nora I'm quite sure at the moment that's not at all a good idea –

She helps him off.

SCENE 6

Enter IWW DELEGATES *for meeting.* ELIZABETH GURLEY FLYNN *is one of them.*

Chairman Fellow workers: we are here at Daniel De Leon's insistence to discuss the affiliation of the waterside workers – goddammit, didn't he say it was a matter of extreme urgency? So where is he? Where the hell is he? If it comes to that, where's Connolly?

1st Delegate All the way from Chicago two days before christmas and there ain't nobody here who knows anything about why this meeting was convened?

Flynn Now wait a minute, Jim Connolly's sick. He's left all the documents with me to handle it for him. On account of it being right on top of the christmas holiday he wants the whole thing finalised, if we can, with the least delay.

2nd Delegate Shouldn't we wait for De Leon?

3rd Delegate Wait hell for De Leon! It's De Leon made all the racket about dragging us all down here – if he don't turn up, that's *his* funeral. Let's get on with it, we got a quorum.

Chairman You've all read Jim Connolly's recommendation. Any objections?

1st Delegate To the incorporation of twelve thousand new proletarians into the outfit? Objections hell! Pass it through and for God's sake, don't waste no more time!

2nd Delegate Say look here, this meeting was called by De Leon. He must have his reasons. We can't just agree to – –

Flynn Why not? He's not here?

Enter DE LEON.

De Leon Comrade Chairman, my apologies: being under the impression that this meeting was scheduled for January the twelfth – –

Chairman Didn't you get the documentation that was sent to you in Chicago? On representations from certain New York delegates the date was changed –

De Leon At the last minute and I received the notification almost too late. Moreover my train from Chicago was held up by snow. You have not yet taken a vote?

2nd Delegate (*smiles and shakes his head reassuringly at* DE LEON)

De Leon Before we do take a vote, may I request that all those persons present who are not members of the IWW Executive Committee be excluded from our deliberations?

Chairman Elizabeth Flynn was presenting – –

De Leon Comrade Flynn is not a member of this committee, I believe.

Chairman In the enforced absence of Comrade Connolly, who fell sick – –

De Leon And very nearly in the enforced absence of Comrade De Leon? Well? Does the lady intend – –

Flynn The lady as requested is on her way out. I'll be in the lobby if you change your minds.

Exit.

De Leon This project for the affiliation of the waterside workers is by no means what it seems. It is a brainchild of James Connolly. *James Connolly*, unskilled labourer, who five years ago tried to pass himself off to me as a qualified linotype operator, who four years ago nearly demoralised the Socialist Labor Party in the city of Troy, who less than two years ago was instrumental in sabotaging the entire working relationship between the SLP Executive and their own newspaper *The Weekly People* – *James Connolly* whose past record in Irish political circles has been shown to consist entirely of faction, subversion, and the internal destruction of the very party he claims to have founded in Dublin – *James Connolly* who has been proved to be not only an agent of the Jesuit Order – how many of you realise the close contact he had with Cardinal Logue during his recent visit to New York: at every meeting that rapacious prelate attended, the man Connolly was there in the front row! – but also we now know that he is an active agent of the New York police and continually gives information to – –

1st Delegate Look, mister, I tried to hold out till you came to the end of a sentence: but with your sentences – hell. I'll be back in thirty seconds.

De Leon Back? Back from where? Where are you going?

1st Delegate If you gotta go, you gotta go. There's only two places where that can be said of, and one of 'em's the morgue . . .

Exit 1ST DELEGATE

De Leon Where was I? Oh yes. Jesuits. Police. Now the Jesuit Order, as maybe you did not realise, was founded in the sixteenth century by Ignatius Loyola in order to – –

3rd Delegate We really must suspend business while one of our members has left the room.

De Leon Why?

3rd Delegate I was addressing the chair.

Chairman Comrade De Leon, if you don't mind, let's keep it on ice till he gets back.

De Leon But I have a great deal more to say, a very great deal more . . .

Chairman Yeah, that's just it . . .

Ominous silence till 1ST DELEGATE *returns.*

1st Delegate I just been talking to the guys outside!

De Leon You had no business to do that!

1st Delegate Every goddam business! Come on boys, Elizabeth, come on in. Dan De Leon's gonna prove his allegations right now before a wide-open forum of the entire organisation – !

FLYNN *and other IWW Members come in angrily. Fury and turmoil.*

Chairman I am about to make a ruling! I am within my rights as chairman: you will not controvert it! Until Comrade Connolly is in a state of health to reply to these accusations, the business of this meeting has gotta be held over. The National Annual Convention of the IWW will be held in Chicago within a matter of months – why don't you put all your gripes on a *small* piece o' paper, Comrade De Leon, and then see what they look like there? In the meantime, this meeting is adjourned. Merry Christmas.

De Leon Comrade Chairman, I insist. Comrade Chairman, I protest – –

Chairman The meeting is adjourned.

Exeunt all save DE LEON *and* 2ND DELEGATE.

2nd Delegate Dan, are you out of your mind? You gone and put the back up every man and woman in this room the way you handled this.

De Leon You are a member of the Socialist Labor Party. I had counted on your support.

2nd Delegate Yeah, you had it, before you came in the goddam room. After that, like, it didn't strike me, you were putting over an *ideology* . . .

Exeunt.

SCENE 7

The IWW CONVENTION *of 1908. A big banner announcing this.* DELEGATES *enter, confusedly, amid a babel of slogans, snatches of song, voices all round the theatre (and from loudspeakers).* CONNOLLY *is conspicuous, handing out leaflets.*

1st Voice
> To Chicago in the mid-months of nineteen-hundred-o-eight –

2nd Voice
> Make or break, revolution now, revolution tomorrow too late –

3rd Voice
> Revolution through preparation, agitation, education, my ass –

4th Voice
> Revolution through nuth'n but the surge of the swell of the mass
> Of the rage of the deprived proletariat – we are here:
> America walk in fear!

General Voices
> Walk in dread, walk in fear,
> Walk in terror of the present time
> That men turned round and said no longer, 'Buddy can you
>   spare a dime?'
> But, 'Buddy can we spare your goddam life!'

3rd Voice
> Lemme tell you from now on there ain't nobody safe!

2nd Voice The Western Federation of Miners was broken away from us by the treachery of the AF of L –

4th Voice The Socialist Party of America does nuth'n but play lousy electoral politics with the organisation, our men is starving in the streets of Pittsburgh, starving, and all they can do for us is promise us paradise for the sake of a lousy vote to run Gene Debs for President.

3rd Voice The Socialist Labor Party don't want no kinda action except all according to the rules and regulations of two-three kraut textbooks Dan De Leon keeps in his hip pocket –

1st Voice (*sings*)
> Hallelujah I'm a bum –

General Voices (*sing*)
> With nuth'n to lose –
> Do we do what we're told
> Or do what we choose?
>
> Do we lie down and fight
> Or rise up and die
> Hallelujah we got here
> And we're all going sky-high . . . !

Connolly From all corners of the world, and the English language sits in their mouths like a hot coal in a pan of water – with their blankets and their dixie-cans and their backs bent and their feet twisted from hanging on like spider-monkeys from the bogies of the freight-cars. The working class and the employing class have nothing in common – and these men here today have so crowded in with such rage into their convention that I cannot believe they can ever get out of it without throwing away almost everything brought them together in the first place. They begin by throwing away the very framework of their procedure – –

Chairman Order, fellow workers, order – we gotta have order here; we gotta make ourselves heard, dammit! It has been moved – it has been moved that the minutes of last year's Convention be read in accordance with – –

Voices No minutes, no minutes, no minutes! Can that bullshit, man, get on with it, get on with what we come for!

Chairman Okay okay, so we bow to the will of the meeting. We got one crucial business that I know and you all know has gotta be settled today and that is – –

Voices Get the politicians out of it – spring ourselves clear of the goddam intellectuals – crack the eggheads outa the outfit – we're proletarians here or nuth'n – Industrial *Workers* of the World so let's have some workers' action – ! *Etcetera* ...

Chairman Just ain't no good going on, boys, without we do it *orderly*! Minutes or no minutes, we just gotta have a motion down—so who's gonna propose it?

Enter DE LEON. *Boos. A few cheers.*

De Leon Comrade Chairman –

3rd Voice Will ya can that *comrade* bullshit! We're one hundred per cent Americans here and we don't want no fucking European faggot-talk: 'fellow-worker' is the word we use, Dan, and you shape it up our way or you ship out, professor!

De Leon Am I going to be heard or not?

Chairman Willya lissen what the man says! He's gotta right to be heard like you've all gotta right to be heard – you've elected me here to ensure that you get that right! Okay. We keep it reasonable or this chair as of now by me is vacated ... Dan De Leon of the Socialist Labor Party has the floor.

De Leon *James Connolly* – of the New York Building and Construction Workers' local – I have demanded the dismissal of that man Connolly from his post! I am appalled he is still here with his sectarian Irish propaganda in his hand! I have consistently and unequivocally published evidence of his treachery to the movement and I demand before any other business Is concluded that this convention examine his so-called credentials and take action thereupon.

Elizabeth Flynn Can we have please a statement of the credentials of Professor De Leon?

De Leon I am not a professor! In the context of this convention I am a . . . I am a . . . Comrade Chairman, if my credentials over the past twenty years in the socialist movement are not recollected the length and breadth of this great nation, there seems little I can do at this late stage to refresh your memory . . .

Voices Answer, answer – !

De Leon I am a member of the IWW by virtue of my status as –

3rd Voice As a company director!

De Leon That is absolutely untrue! I am the managing editor of a socialist newspaper – –

4th Voice He's the only one he can trust down there to keep his fingers outa the till!

De Leon Which is and always has been conducted upon principles of – –

Flynn Which union do your printers belong to?

De Leon I myself am a member of a labour-organisation – –

3rd Voice You yourself refused to join the IWW printers' local!

De Leon That was only because – –

Connolly Because you were already a member of quite another local – the store and office workers, were you not, which does not happen to be affiliated to this organisation? It's a technical legalistic non-intellectual issue. A ruling from the chair, please, yes or no?

Chairman Ain't no doubt about it: he shows up his card of membership of an IWW union or he quits this hall pronto.

De Leon I am here ex officio as an elected representative of the Socialist Labor Party –

Chairman Which for sure ain't no trade union.

De Leon Which was recognised at the founding convention of nineteen hundred and five as part and parcel of the structure of the Industrial Workers of the World –

Voices This is nineteen oh eight, not nineteen oh five – get wise, man. What happened in nineteen oh five is dead and deep down under – we ain't bound by none of last year's structure, tear it out – ! (*etcetera* . . .)

De Leon I'm within my rights to demand a vote.

Chairman I question that. But you can have one. Representatives of political parties have an ex-officio place at the IWW Convention. Those in favour? . . . Those agin? . . . Two-thirds agin. One-third in favour. Sorry, friend, just ain't your day. Come back again next year with your little pink card in the heel of your sock and show it to the man at the door.

Connolly Before he goes, my own position. I'd be obliged for a vote on that. If people really believe I acquired this card of membership under false pretences as a detective, or a priest, I am more than content to take the majority decision and surrender it, here and now.

Chairman Okay, we'll make it regular. Vote of confidence, here and now, upon the credentials of Jim Connolly. Those in favour that he's on the level?

. . . Those who think that he's a rat and should be druv back into his hole? . . . Okay, justice triumphs. Keep your seat, Jim, guess you've earned it, you're one of us, boy . . . We get to business.

A short pause as DE LEON *ostentatiously leaves the body of the hall (but remains where he can observe the ensuing business) amid boos and a few cheers.*

In the preamble to our constitution we have the sentence that pronounces the necessity for economic as well as political action to achieve our ends. There's a motion put down to delete the word 'political'. Proposer? Big Bill Haywood.

Haywood (*amid a storm of cheering*) Just so long as we can keep ourselves together as an organisation of industrial workers, with the power to strike, the power to picket, the power to sabotage inside the plant, we are capable at a moment's notice of pulling out every man that shovels coal and greases wheels from San Francisco to New York: and the whole bad edifice of Wall Street finance-capital both knows that power and trembles at it! But let the political parties – whether capitalist or so-called socialist – get their hands on our united strength, they will strip us off like onions, skin by skin, to enable them the better to trade vote against vote and so slip into their seats in state and national legislature and fix themselves a good career! Get rid of that damnfool preamble and make use of your huge energies to totally bankrupt the plutocracy! 'Cos there ain't no other way but that, and that's it and I'm finished . . .

Chairman Hold it, now, order! Didn't I tell you, I will have order! So let's hear the opposer.

2ND DELEGATE *from Scene 6 rises to oppose.*

Opposer So if only the union's big enough, it can grind America to a halt . . . so we starve . . . so what then? There still ain't no way we can actually *run* the goddam country! I quote Karl Marx: 'The proletariat will use its political supremacy to wrest, by degrees, all capital from the bourgeoisie, to centralise all instruments of production in the hands of the State – i.e.: of the proletariat organised as the ruling class – and to increase the total of productive forces as rapidly as possible!' Yeah, you threw out Dan De Leon, but I tell you, without De Leon and the nation-wide party newspaper he edited for this movement, the expression of our struggle would be utterly denied to us!

Chairman Those in favour of deleting the word *political* from the preamble of our constitution? . . . Those against? . . . Motion carried. The word's deleted: and that's it.

De Leon
From now on the IWW has not one chance on God's earth
To beget the revolution and bring it forth to triumphant birth.

He stalks out and through the DELEGATES. *A moment of dead silence.
Exeunt.*

SCENE 8

*The presidential election campaign of 1908, Balloons, posters, tickertape,
etcetera.*

Enter REPORTERS. *They speak rapidly to the audience while all the election
razzmatazz goes on behind.*

1st Reporter Come on come on come on roll up roll up and leave aside these
chicken-shit minority preoccupations. The people of America nineteen-
hundred-and-eight under God are about to elect their new President!
Endorsed by the outgoing incumbent Teddy Roosevelt, for the Republicans runs William Taft! The year of depression and slump is
finally lifting, the Republican Party stands revealed as the precursor of
ever-increasing prosperity for more and more Americans!

2nd Reporter For the Democrats William Jennings Bryan repeats his clarion
call 'You shall not crucify mankind upon a cross of gold!' and brands
the obstructive financial practices of the cartels and monopoly trusts.

1st Reporter The obstructive financial practices of the cartels and monopoly
trusts have no more ardent antagonist than the remarkable third candidate – Eugene Debs of the Socialist Party of America. In the election of
nineteen hundred and four Debs ran a campaign in opposition to the
big parties that brought him nearly half-a-million votes: this time he
intends to more than double that figure. We have seen the repudiation of
political action by the IWW in Chicago. Will we now see the justification
by the SPA of the very stance so many of its trade unionist members have
already renounced? For there's no doubt that in their thousands the
individual Wobblies flock to the Debs bandwagon and urge him forward
to the polls!

2nd Reporter This is the greatest, most spectacular national campaign ever
launched in the name of socialism – with a locomotive and a sleeping-
car, hired at the unprecedented and almost unattainable cost of twenty
thousand dollars, Eugene Debs has left Chicago on the first leg of his
coast-to-coast, whistle-stop tour, the scarlet flag of his amazing doctrine
flying proudly from the pilot and the smoke-stack of his aptly-named
'Red Special'!

Enter GOMPERS.

Gompers If Debs gets one million votes, then the Democrat-Republican two-
party system will be thrown into the melting-pot and maybe next time
round in nineteen twelve we're gonna see but one candidate running for
capitalism and one candidate run for socialism, and the entire delicate
balance between organised labour – *my* organised labour – and the
representatives of big business will be thrown into the melting-pot. The

American working man is *not* a socialist – he is an unfulfilled capitalist – and to save for him his hopes and dreams I add my voice – 'Stop Debs!'

Enter GRABITALL *and* BOSSES.

Grabitall and Bosses
> Stop Debs!
> Vote for Taft, vote for Bryan
> Vote for *either*, vote for *or* –

Gompers Hell no, not Taft, vote Bryan and sweep the floor!

Grabitall and Bosses
> Just so we all know
> Devil Debs is shown the door!
> Stop Debs!

Gompers (*sings*)
> All the bums called Eugene in nineteen-eight
> You'd better get movin or you're gonna be late
> If the old locomotive don't run outa steam
> You're gonna drive slap-bang through the American dream!

Grabitall and Bosses (*sing*)
> Eugene Debs, he's mounted to the cabin
> Eugene Debs with his orders in his hand
> Eugene Debs with his German ideology
> On the great Red Special to the promised land!

DEBS *and his election team, as though conveyed on the train, pass round and over the stage, waving red flags.*

Enter CONNOLLY.

Connolly In this election I helped Debs. Not on the Red Special but on my own appropriate speaking tour in what they call the Pope's backyard – the Irish communities of the East Coast, hoeing hard at the potato-rows of the traditional Democrat vote. Socialism . . . ? Well, they *listened*. But to Debs they did more than listen. Why they hailed that man like John the Baptist . . .

Debs The capitalists who rule America understand one language and one language only – the language of power! Give me one million votes and already we begin to hold that power in our own hands! The Socialist Party aims to compel Congress to put an end to court injunctions against strikes and lawful picketing: to enact laws affirming the statutory eight-hour day: and to enforce liability and safety regulations upon every industry in the USA! With that for a beginning the working class has the road open for its own industrial triumph, through the unions, to destroy the evil monster of finance-capital exploitation! The Red Special runs west – Des Moines, Muscatine, Corning, from Iowa into Nebraska: Omaha . . .

Gompers (*sings*)

> Pour on the water, shovel on the coal
> Put God's own country under alien control
> He's comin for your dollars and he's comin for your wife
> And he's comin for *you* for the rest of your life!

Grabitall and Bosses (*sing*)

> Eugene Debs, he's mounted to the cabin
> Eugene Debs with his orders in his hand
> Eugene Debs, with his German ideology
> On the great Red Special to the promised land!

Connolly Whether or no the depression, as claimed by the Republicans, was in fact easing up, the IWW proved unable to pay me even my starvation stipend of eighteen dollars a week. From the SPA in the full flush of its election fever I could earn enough speaking-fees to keep my family alive for a wee while longer. Moreover the party have given me nation-wide facilities for the distribution of *The Harp*.

Debs Denver, Colorado: Leadville, Colorado: Santa Barbara, California . . . Did I hear someone say that a vote for socialism is a vote thrown away? That's right, friend, that's right: don't vote for freedom – you might not get it. Vote for slavery – you have a cinch on that. Ye gods, but these are pregnant days! San Diego, Los Angeles, Spokane, Billings Montana – the heartland of the Wobbly country . . .

Gompers (*sings*)

> Toot on the whistle and ring on the bell
> There ain't no heaven and there ain't no hell
> He's gonna drag you down and level you out
> And your hard-earned wages goin up the spout!

Grabitall and Bosses (*sing*)

> Eugene Debs, he's mounted to the cabin
> Eugene Debs with his orders in his hand
> Eugene Debs with his German ideology
> On the great Red Special to the promised land!

Connolly The Socialist Party of America includes all, expels none: but Debs as their candidate talks sound industrial unionism in every city where he speaks. I can do no better than stay with him.

Debs St Paul Minnesota, Duluth, Chicago, Toledo, Rochester, New York City . . .

1st Reporter The greatest political meeting ever held in this city! If, as Roosevelt says, the adherents of this doctrine are undesirable citizens, an enormous number are going to have to be deported before this nation regains its health.

Debs Philadelphia, Camden, Newark, Pittsburgh, Harpers Ferry . . . The work begun here by John Brown is now carried on by the Socialist Party of America. We today are the true, the only, abolitionists of slavery!

And so back to Chicago, with my voice so weak with speaking I can scarcely be heard . . .

Gompers (*sings*)
> Oh it's beans and bacon for every man
> And a two-dollar charge when you go to the can
> If you can't pay your way, boy, don't you mind –
> There's a train full of bullshit on the socialist line!

Grabitall and Bosses (*sing*)
> Eugene Debs, he's mounted to the cabin
> Eugene Debs, with his orders in his hand
> Eugene Debs with his German ideology
> On the great Red Special to the promised land . . .

1st Reporter And the result? William Taft becomes President.

Gompers Yeah: with the Republicans I can maybe do a deal . . .

1st Reporter William Jennings Bryan has been heavily defeated.

Gompers Sure, Bryan was just a crazy man – a small-town, shyster lawyer with crank notions about currency. That guy wouldn't know the difference between an affiliated craft union and a goddam temperance guild. Good riddance . . .

1st Reporter And Eugene Debs – ?

Gompers His million votes – ?

Grabitall and Bosses His power of opinion to lobby Congress into ruinous legislation – ?

1st Reporter Less than half-a-million votes – hardly better than he did in nineteen oh four . . .

Debs The campaign is ended. But the loyal support given me in every part of the country expressed the true spirit of socialist comradeship, which is the making of our movement and which will sustain it through every ordeal until it is finally triumphant.

Connolly Of course the effect of the ballot is limited by the degree of democratic supervision which can be exercised over the actual boxes. For instance in Terre Haute where Debs himself voted –

Debs Not one vote for the socialists was registered in that precinct. Am I supposed to believe in a moment of amnesia I cast my name for William Taft?

Exeunt all save CONNOLLY. GRABITALL *and* BOSSES *go out in a posture of mock innocence and giggling at* DEBS'*s disclosure . . .*

SCENE 9

Connolly After the defeat, the discussion of the reason therefor.
> Reordering of the battalions for the next battle in the long long war.

He withdraws.

Enter DEBS.

Debs   Health broken, spirit for the time being diminished,
I walk gloomily aside while recrimination rolls over and fro –

Enter HILLQUIT, HAYWOOD *and other* SPA MEMBERS *to take their seats in committee –* HILLQUIT *in chair,* HAYWOOD *and* 1ST MEMBER *on left,* 2ND *and* 3RD MEMBERS *on right.*

I am sure you guys will know
Where to find me if you want me the moment you're finished.

DEBS *sits down well away from them with a bottle.*

Hillquit Why didn't the working-class vote match up to the mass support given Comrade Debs on his tour, hey? I'll tell you why, plain as the nose on your faces, because the American worker has either gone crazy lone ranging with the non-political Wobblies, or else he sticks with Sam Gompers of the AF of L – and Gompers backed Bryan, who promised a whole load of phoney reform. Add to that, with the slump, three-quarters of the proletarian vote had left home in the depression to look for work somewheres else, so their names were on no voting register.

1st Member Gene Debs talked fine about revolution and industrial unionism: but there was more than Gene Debs to the campaign and the people knew it. Yeah, a working-class party? What the hell does a man think when he sees the potential socialist president of the USA backed by a crowd of college professors, society sob-sisters, and old-style baptist evangelists?

Haywood I'll tell you what he thinks – he thinks, 'With those guys in the White House, what chance has a regular two-fisted immigrant Yid like Karl Marx even to get his toecaps past the guard at the gate!'

3rd Member I don't wanna hear nuth'n, ever again, about Karl Marx and his two fists! If I wanted any saints I'd prefer to turn catholic and buy 'em up wholesale!

2nd Member Immigrant – yeah, you said it!

3rd Member It's the yellow peril on the west coast that chaws 'em up the worst. Why, there's Chinamen and Japs by the million coming in to San Francisco any day of the week. Get that herd to join a union, let alone a political party? Goddam lunacy to let them in, and it's high time our voice was heard on it!

Haywood You ever worked with Japs?

3rd Member I know enough about them, and their rate of propagation, yeah and the number of wives and concubines they're allowed to have back home! Do you know, an oriental, on one little saucer of rice per day, will – –

Haywood I said, you ever worked with Japs? I have: in the mining camps: and I can tell you, in a no-holds-barred labour struggle there ain't no better fighter in the world!

1st Member If I'm told the Jap will carry the socialist banner in a place where the white man fails, then all hail to the Jap – let him carry it for me!

2nd Member And let you carry the can, comrade, for every vote you're gonna lose! Oh, Sam Gompers knows his onions – as a matter of pragmatic tactics, we simply don't dare to alienate that guy's membership – four-square white Americans and the only possible bedrock for a socialist campaign!

Uproar. Right and left bellow incoherently and shake their fists at each other.

Hillquit Comrades, for God's sake! We're all falling apart. Okay, so it's time to offer up some sort of compromise. We gotta get rid of these right-wing fool arguments about saucers of rice and the oriental birth-rate – that's not socialism – nothing less than Ku-klux-klannery, and the sooner we forget it was ever spoken, the better. On the other hand . . .

Debs (*lurches to his feet, and speaking to the audience*) On the other hand . . . ?

Hillquit There's no doubt the race question *is* a sore point. We already have enough problems with the negro in the south . . . Hey, how about this – 'The Socialist Party of America favors all legislative measures tending to prevent the immigration of' – wait for it – 'strike-breakers and contract-laborers brought about by the employing classes for the purpose of weakening the determination of American workers'? You get the tactic – lay the blame on the boss class: and emphasise the inability of these backward ethnic elements to understand trade union principles.

Haywood My God, but I just told you – –

Debs (*lurches into the meeting*) Unsocialistic, reactionary, outrageous . . . The revolutionary character of our party must be preserved in its integrity at all cost . . .

He lurches out again.

Hillquit We take a vote on it? In favour? Against? Motion tied. Casting vote from the chair – in favour. Motion passed. Okay, so what next? Question of attitude toward trade unions. The IWW has been so all-fired hostile to the AF of L, I guess we've got no option but to take stock, and that fast.

2nd Member We don't want to go so far as to *repudiate* the Wobblies.

3rd Member We don't want to go so far as to repudiate *anybody*! Least of all Sam Gompers – as a matter of tactical pragmatism. But Gompers ain't no socialist, and we can't just endorse his outfit, outa hand. Not just yet.

Haywood Sonofabitch! You mean that in due time you believe you *can* endorse it!

2nd Member Now wait a minute, he didn't say – –

Haywood I heard what he said!

Hillquit If we don't repudiate Gompers and we don't repudiate the Wobblies, it means in effect we decide to take no position on the trade union question. Maybe that's just exactly the position that we should take. So why don't we ease up on this theoretical controversy and bad blood, hey? Get some regular all-American propaganda put over. We've got newspapers and lecture-tours and ginger-group organisers set and ready to go all over the country. Say, there's thousands more read our papers than dared to put the vote in for us: we gotta get hold of those guys through the medium of the printed word and just boost 'em to the polls next time round, what do you say? Slow and systematic education of the working class, *education* – so let's get on with it! Gene, we've finished.

Debs Yeah, I heard. We have already catered far too much to the AF of L – a halt will have to be called. So for God's sake, boys, just you call it . . .

Exit.

Haywood

From now on the SPA has not one chance on God's earth
To beget the revolution and bring it forth to triumphant birth.

Exit, followed by all except 3RD MEMBER.

3rd Member Okay, so where are all these party workers we got feeding their face on our goddam payroll? Hey, you there – Comrade Connolly –
Enter CONNOLLY.
Here's your newspapers – get 'em sold, willya, quick, and then go to Philadelphia – there's a lecture-date fixed up for you – go tell 'em the good news about 'Workers of the World Unite' – you can draw your expenses from my secretary before the banks close. Hey, after Philadelphia, how about Tucson Arizona, an'a whole load o' dates way up toward Montana – boy, in this outfit you sure get to go places!

Exit, leaving CONNOLLY *with a great pile of papers.*

SCENE 10

Enter LILLIE.

Lillie (*addresses the audience without reference to* CONNOLLY)
While he goes to Arizona there's a public holiday in New York.
Would you believe my daughter Nora and the young people with her at work
Are actually made able to take me on a holiday picnic, a trip by boat
Up the Hudson River, a whole day to do nothing in a green park
Except rest and enjoy ourselves and do nothing from morning till dark . . .
And some of this she pays for and some of it *I* pay for and none of it comes from him –

Because at last from his regular wage we can cover all that we
  need in the home
And what's over is extra – we can spend it however we like:
Do you know it's the first holiday I've ever had in the whole of
  my life . . . ?

Exit LILLIE.

Connolly Twenty-one dollars per week, three more than I got from the
  Wobblies, that's it –
Plus travelling expenses, commission from sales of papers, not a
  bit
Good complaining that the work is a repetitive drag
So long as I can kid myself that in the end, deep down in the
  bottom of the bag
I can grope for and find and haul out into the sunlight glare
The true jewel of revolution, like Venus from the ocean,
Long-legged, wild-eyed, red-gold-haired bare
Terror to the closed mind, the closed-down forehead, the envious
  shoulders that stoop
The shadow of capitalist rule over the length of this working
  world . . . small hope,
I know that; all the smaller for the decisions that have just been
  made.
Yet here I am, the wheels turn round, the pistons plunge and
  slide
Day in, day out, the locomotive blows for the climbing of one
  more grade –
So much paper, so many acres of print:
But how much power in all these words so fabulously spent
And sent about, perhaps read, perhaps not read,
But understood?
No good
To talk about it: act.
This literature is a fact.

The titles of it alone would fill a graveyard – *The Appeal to Reason, The
Worker, The Socialist Weekly Bulletin, The Socialist Party Official
Bulletin, The Socialist, The Social Democratic Herald, The Workers' Call,*
pamphlets moreover – *The Socialist Campaign Book, Capitalist Union or
Labor Unions, which? Party Politics and the Trade Unions, The Attack on
the Trade Unions, Shall the Unions go into Politics?* – translations more-
over of the publications of the permitted immigrant federations:
Bohemian, Finnish, Italian, Polish, Scandinavian, South Slavic, Lettish,
Hungarian – add to this all my own stuff – *The Harp, Erin's Hope* – oh
my God, Erin's hope . . .

> Out of Ireland, what hope? Out of Ireland where is the horn
> That will tear the heavens asunder and proclaim that at last is
>   born
> In Belfast or in Dublin the achieved fulfilment of our mortal need?
> Seven years in this great wilderness where nothing will breed
> But dry bones,
> Thorns and broken stone . . .

Larkin (*voice off*) I had a mission in Belfast! To create a trade union among perhaps the most backward industrial people in the whole of western Europe – the carters and coal-fillers and dock labourers of the swarming sectarian slums.

Connolly (*suddenly roused from his gloom*) James Larkin – I'd never met him – he came over from Liverpool after I had left for America – could it be that this man – ?

Larkin (*voice off*) I created that union, and I brought them on strike: for the first time for over a century protestant and catholic were united in defence of their rights as human beings! No, we were not going to be beasts any longer – we were to rouse the working classes out of their slough of despond and with the microbe of discontent in our blood to lift ourselves up on to the peak of Mount Optimism!

Still orating, he strides in, but a good distance from CONNOLLY, *rather as though he is descried in a vision.*

And the result, the entrenched leaders of the bureaucratic craft union, from their headquarters in Britain, struck with terror lest our revolt should develop into revolution, dragged me back out of the struggle and demanded I should repudiate the very militancy I had set aflame. For such runagates, I will defy them! We will begin our *own* union – the Irish Transport Workers – for the unskilled casual wage-slaves, whatever their religion, in Belfast, Dublin, Cork, and every corner of the land! An independent Irish union for an independent Irish nation – One Big Union One Big Strike – and let the cross-channel labour fakers go to hell where they belong!

Connolly Why does it have to be him in Belfast and not me . . . ?

Larkin James Connolly, why does it have to be me in Belfast and not you? Come home, man, you are *required* here!

Exit LARKIN.

SCENE 11

Connolly Oh sure, if my old comrades in the Socialist Party of Ireland could break into the bank on College Green when the cashier was not looking and get hold of the passage-money, and send it – within a week I'd be on my way . . .

Enter LILLIE.

Lillie How many letters have you sent to O'Brien in Dublin to find out what he can do for you?

Connolly Would you have me count the wild geese in their migration to the tide-filled sloblands?

Lillie How many answers have you had?

Connolly I am waiting for but *one* answer – I have told him if I get it, future generations of little Connollys will rise up and call him blessed . . .

Lillie   In Scotland he began, in Ireland carried it on –
In America it had seemed I could make for him his secure home:
From America if the wild women of revolution in his mind
Call him forth and he must go, I will not stay behind –
To turn the whole world upside-down
Is a task for no fixed citizen of an enclosed and guarded town . . .

Letter appears, as though by magic – a sort of deus-ex-machina *episode.*

Connolly and Lillie (*breathlessly, together*) It's the letter – and it says – ?

Voice of the Letter
    James Larkin is in prison on a trumped-up charge
    We must have Connolly, till Larkin is at large
    All Ireland quakes and shudders, revolution is at hand
    James Connolly, come home to your own proper land!
    Your fare will be paid, your position assured
    At last your Irish comrades send authentic urgent word:
    Don't look back, leave your wife to follow after –
    The whole new world of socialism breaks to birth across the
        water!

Connolly If I do not at once at last go home once more
    This huge America will kill my heart
    And nail my worn-out body to the floor –
    In nineteen-hundred-ten, July,
    I wave my children and my wife good-bye
    Aloft aboard the boat to cross the sea –
    So soon, so soon you follow after me. . . .

Exeunt severally.

SCENE 12

Enter GRABITALL – *wearing round his stars-and-stripes top hat a mass of red, white, and blue ribbons like a mane falling on to his shoulders.*

Grabitall Mr Gompers – !

Enter GOMPERS.

Gompers Mr President, Mr Senator, Mr Congressman, sir – oh, Mr Inter-locutor, please sir, call me Sam!

Grabitall Sam, boy – call me Uncle! Well, hell, goldarn it, Sam, what are we gonna do about this Panama Canal?

Gompers Build it, Uncle, build it good.

Grabitall On an eight-hour day at a guaranteed minimum wage? Boy, you push too far!

Gompers In that climate, for the white labour, just ain't no alternative, Uncle.

Grabitall In that climate, if the white labour don't sweat twice as hard as the greasers, then nobody, nohow's gonna do any work at all. Unlimited hours, Sam, and the wage rates raise proportional.

Gompers No! No, sir, Uncle, there just ain't no deal forthcoming.

Grabitall Say, hell, Sam, now look at it this way – hey! Say, what d'you say, Sam, we're gonna *do* with that damn canal?

Gompers Why, Uncle, ship the navy through it – the United States Navy, ocean-to-ocean, in control of the entire hemisphere!

Grabitall And do we have the navy, boy, to control the entire hemisphere?

Gompers Uncle, we must build it, we must build it goddam good!

Grabitall On a guaranteed eight-hour day in every government-contract shipyard!

Gompers Uncle: it's a deal . . . ! Hot dog – copper-bottomed – for the con-struction of the canal you can lay down your own terms – !

Grabitall And by nineteen fourteen the keels of our new ships will be breasting every tideline from Buenos Aires to El Salvador –

He sings:

> So soon in every Dago port our cruisers drop their anchor
> To set on land with bag in hand the modest Yankee banker –

Enter BOSSES.

Bosses (*sing*)
> He will not come with sword and gun nor buccaneering forces:
> We keep those hid till every bid lies on the floor of auction.

Grabitall and Bosses (*sing*)
> Bananas in the jungle and tobacco on the plain
> And copper in the mountains bursting out at every vein
> The oil that gushes upward will come down again like rain
> For the NEW CONQUISTADORS!

GOMPERS *is marshalling a line of* WORKERS, *whom he dresses in a long stars-and-stripes cloth: the head of the line clutches the waist of* GRABITALL, *thus forming a Chinese-style dancing dragon, which begins to perambulate the theatre in time to the music.*

All (*sing*)

        Glory, glory hallelujah
        Dollar bills will live for ever
        Every man a Rockefeller
        With the NEW CONQUISTADORS!

Grabitall (*sings*)

        I stuck my finger up a Dago's hole
        And the Dago said 'God bless my soul –
        Revolu – Revolu – Revolu – Revolution.'

Bosses (*sing*)

        Oh Diego, what a curious word you use:
        For the revolution you will get is the one that we will choose –
        Your colonels and your justices from us will take their pay
        And twice the money they receive they'll give back every day.
        Oh Diego, you know we cannot lose:
        For there never was a dollar yet you ever did refuse!

MARINES *march across with rifles and flags.*

Marines (*sing*)

        And if any should find reason to doubt us or mistrust
        Remember in due season how much the Spaniards lost
        At Manila and Havana in eighteen ninety eight
        When the old imperial Europe heard the thunder at the gate!

Gompers and Grabitall (*sing*)

        When Capital and Labour are at last identified
        In the gathering of profit from the world both far and wide
        The power of our great nation will be felt on every side
        Through the NEW CONQUISTADORS!

All (*sing*)

        Glory glory Hallelujah
        Here we come to take you over
        Bow your heads and follow after
        The NEW CONQUISTADORS . . . !

Exeunt.

END OF PART FOUR

Margaretta D'Arcy and John Arden

The Non-Stop Connolly Show

A Dramatic Cycle of Continuous Struggle in Six Parts

Part One: Boyhood 1868–1889

James Connolly, born among the Irish in Edinburgh, can find no
work, so joins the Army and is sent to Ireland. He discovers
Irish nationalism and international socialism: he discovers a
wife: he discovers his political destiny. He determines to go
elsewhere.

Part Two: Apprenticeship 1889–1896

James Connolly, in Edinburgh once more and married, gains
experience in the pioneer socialist movement. He seeks political
office and fails to find it: he seeks to earn a living and fails
likewise. He determines to go elsewhere.

Part Three: Professional 1896–1903

Act I: A Movement with Some Purpose.

James Connolly becomes a political organiser in Dublin and
founds the Irish Socialist Republican Party. He meets the New
Ireland of the literary renaissance and disrupts the royal Jubilee.

Act II: Alarums and Excursions.

James Connolly, in Dublin, leads the Irish Socialist Republican
Party in militant opposition to British imperialism and the Boer
War. He is criticised by Keir Hardie of the British Labour
movement.

Act III: Outmanoeuvred.

James Connolly is rejoiced to find the Irish Socialist Republican
Party recognised by the Socialist International. Rosa Luxemburg
– in controversy with Kautsky – throws doubt upon Connolly's
views of Irish nationhood. The Irish Socialist Republican Party
throws doubt upon his views of political priorities. He determines
to go elsewhere.

Part Four: The New World 1903–1910

Act I: Into the Party.

James Connolly emigrates to the United States. He joins the
Socialist Labor Party, led by Daniel De Leon. He is frustrated
by its doctrinaire sectarianism.

Act II: Out of the Party.

James Connolly greets with enthusiasm the Industrial Workers
of the World, believing them to be the great new revolutionary
force. He forms the Irish Socialist Federation among immigrants
in the USA. Unable to accommodate himself to De Leon's
control of the Socialist Labor Party, he determines to pursue
his politics elsewhere.

Act III: Forward to the Revolution . . . ?

James Connolly, as IWW Organiser, struggles against odds in
New York. He helps the presidential election campaign of
Eugene Debs. He becomes a paid worker for the Socialist Party
of America. He determines to go elsewhere.

Part Five: The Great Lockout 1910–1914

Act I: Donnybrook Fair.

James Connolly returns to Ireland and its furious political and
trade union confusions. He meets James Larkin, who sends him
to Belfast to organise the new Irish Transport Workers' Union.
He has ideological clashes with William Walker of the Northern
Ireland labour movement.

Act II: Keir Hardie's Promise.

James Connolly continues his work in Ireland for the labour
movement. The Irish Labour Party is founded. The Dublin
Employers' Federation is founded. The 'Great Lockout' is
imposed: Larkin, aided by Connolly, responds with a general
strike.

Act III: Once More Go Down To Hell.

James Connolly sees the Dublin General Strike collapse when
the British trade union leadership fails to respond to the demands
of its rank and file that the Irish workers be given positive
support. The Irish Citizen Army is formed. The Irish National
Volunteers are formed. The climate of violence intensifies.

Part Six: World War and the Rising 1914–1916

Prologue: King Conaire and the Prohibitions.

In ancient times good King Conaire saved the country from its enemies by fighting them against all odds: even though the circumstances of the battle were contrary to the ritual prohibitions prescribed by his Druids.

Act I: Clouds of War.

James Connolly confronts the aftermath of the great lockout in Dublin. The Irish constitutional crisis brings fears of civil war, combining with the threat of a general strike in Britain. International imperial rivalries simultaneously intensify.

Act II: World War to Civil War.

James Connolly sees international socialism collapse in the face of the outbreak of the world war. Resolute in his opposition to imperialism in all its forms, he seeks desperately for allies – in particular from among the members of the Irish Republican Brotherhood within the National Volunteers.

Act III: The Rising.

James Connolly brings the Irish Citizen Army into the Rising of Easter 1916: and thereby becomes the first working-class leader to enter the world conflict in the cause of socialism. He is compelled to surrender to superior force: and is shot to death.